THE WICKED TRICKS OF TILL OWLYGLASS

THE WICKED TRICKS OF
TILL OWLYGLASS

*For Harold and remembering Connie
who introduced me to Till; and Geraldine,
Joe, Naomi, Eddie, Laura and Isaac*
M.R.

*For Amelia and David with
appreciation for all the patient support
and encouragement*
F.W.

THE WICKED TRICKS OF TILL OWLYGLASS

Michael Rosen

Illustrated by
Fritz Wegner

WALKER BOOKS
AND SUBSIDIARIES
LONDON · BOSTON · SYDNEY · AUCKLAND

FOREWORD

It seems as if the Till Owlyglass stories
have been around for more than
five hundred years. They started out in
the lands that we now call Germany
and his name there is Till Eulenspiegel.

He is still very popular there and
for a while he was well-known in the
English-speaking world too.

I love the stories so much that I wanted
to share them with you. If you like them,
I hope that you will pass them on too.

Michael Rosen

CONTENTS

THE FIRST DAY

WHEN WE HEAR HOW TILL OWLYGLASS
WAS BAPTISED THREE TIMES IN ONE DAY,
AND HOW HE DECEIVED HIS FATHER
WHILE RIDING ON A HORSE

A long time ago, when I was young, I went to stay in Germany with my mum and dad and brother. Mum and Dad were very busy in the mornings, working, so me and my brother were often left on our own until dinner time.

Most of the time we had to stay in our room and play or read. After a while, as I am sure you can imagine, we got bored. And you know what happens when children get bored – they get into trouble. And that's just what happened to us.

There was the time we climbed out of the

window onto the roof and dropped bits of bread on the heads of the people walking along below. There was the time we did pretend-flying and my brother did his pretend-flying off the end of the bed and landed on his face. And there was the time we played football with my dad's shoes and one of the shoes went flying out of the window.

We got into so much trouble my mum and dad just didn't know what to do. In the end, someone helped them. It was the caretaker. He had a father, a very old man called Horst. The caretaker said, "My father will stop them being bad. The best thing to do with those boys is to take them to see old Horst." And so, one morning, that's what happened.

Can you imagine it, me and my brother being taken off to see a strange old man we had never met? The caretaker took us downstairs to his flat and up to Old Man Horst's door. The caretaker called out at the door. We heard a gruff old voice come from inside. The caretaker opened the door, we went in, the door closed behind us and we were on our own in this small dark room. Old Man Horst was sitting on a painted wooden chair with his glasses on. He had one of those floppy moustaches that make men look as if they've got a mop in front of their mouths. He had one hand on the table and one hand on his knee.

"So, you're the two bad little boys we hear so much about," said the old man. We didn't say a thing. "Well, I'm going to stop this, you know. I'm going to cure you. Sit down."

We sat down on a bench. I felt all jumpy inside. "Well," he said, "I can see that you think you're bad. In fact, lots of people think you're bad. But I'll tell you this, little fellows. I know of

someone much, much worse than you two. Do you know who he is?"

"No," said my brother.

"He's called Till Eulenspiegel. Can you say that?"

"Tilloilyshleegle," said my brother.

"In English he has another name," said Old

Man Horst. "Till Owlyglass. Can you say that?"

"Tilly Owlyglass," I said.

"Till Owlyglass," said Horst. "He was the worst boy the world has ever known and he grew to be even worse than worst. Have you ever heard of him?"

"Where does he live?" said my brother, but I was wondering how Old Man Horst was going to stop us being bad. How was he going to cure us?

Old Man Horst laughed. "Till doesn't live anywhere. He lived hundreds and hundreds of years ago. You know, he was so bad that people remember many of the bad things that he did. Do you think an old man like me might know one or two of these bad things?"

I nodded.

"And do you think two bad little boys like you might want to know about someone like this?"

This time I could see that he had a smile on his face and there were creases round his eyes behind his glasses. So I nodded quite hard.

"Good," he said. "Where shall I begin? At the beginning, in the middle or at the end?"

I said, "Begin at the beginning."

"Right," said Old Man Horst. And this is how he began.

* * *

Till Owlyglass was born in a little village called Kneitlingen, and right from the very beginning, his life was strange.

In those days every baby was baptised in church. The priest blessed the baby, gave it its name and put a little water on it. And so it was with Till. He was named Till Owlyglass, sprinkled with holy water and then all the friends and neighbours went off to the village inn to have a party, eat a bit, drink a bit, sing a bit, tell jokes and stories and have a good time.

In the evening, when the party broke up, all the villagers strolled out of the inn into the night air and started to make their way home, still singing and laughing.

Till's mum, Mrs Owlyglass, was carrying Till, and she came to the old narrow bridge over the village stream, and, *whoops!* she tripped, she fell, and you can guess what happened. She went rolling into the stream still holding little baby Till.

Mr Owlyglass rushed to help the pair of them out of the water and the mud, and suddenly the night was full of people calling out, "How's Mrs Owlyglass?" "Never mind her, what about the baby?" "Is he breathing?" "Oh, the poor little dear!" "Oooh, look at his muddy nose!" and so on.

Mrs Owlyglass rushed home with Till and straightaway bathed him in a tub of warm water.

"Well, well, well," said Mr Owlyglass, when all the excitement and worry was over. "This son of ours is going to turn into someone very special."

"How's that?" said Mrs Owlyglass.

"He's been baptised three times in one day, once by the priest, once in the village stream and once in a hot tub. Not bad going, eh?"

Of course when Till's dad said that, he couldn't have known just how right he was. Till would turn out to be very special – but maybe not the kind of special most mothers or fathers would like.

* * *

Old Man Horst stopped and waited. "Shall I go on?" he said.

"Oh yes," I said. "What happened to him when he was a little boy?"

"Aha," said Horst, and went on with the story.

* * *

Right from the very beginning Till behaved like a naughty monkey, pulling his father's beard, jumping out of his bed in the middle of the night, climbing into neighbours' houses and making rude noises under the table, and when they weren't looking, putting vinegar in their drinks. He was what you'd call "a right little shocker".

Soon neighbours and friends were coming to see Mr and Mrs Owlyglass to complain about

Till. "I've never known a child like him." "If he was my son, I'd take a stick to him and beat him till he mended his ways." "If he comes in my house again, I shall give him such a smack, he won't ever forget it." "He put mud in my shoes, you know."

And so it went on, complaint after complaint.

So Till's father had to talk to the boy. He said, "What is all this, son? What's going on? Why do all my friends and neighbours moan about you?"

But Till had an answer to this. "They're lying, Dad," he said. "They just want to get back at you because they're jealous your chickens are laying such good eggs."

Till knew just how to stop his father getting angry with him.

But the trouble went on, and people kept complaining, and in the end Till said to his father, "Look, I'll tell you what, Dad. We'll go out on the horse, you and me together, and you'll see that even though I do nothing to make people angry, they all start their trouble-making just the same."

And this is what they did. Till's father sat on the horse and little Till sat behind him, and whenever they rode past someone, Till stuck out his tongue, pulled faces and put his fingers up his nose.

Straightaway people started shouting, "Look at him, the nasty creature! Oh, I'd love to give that little devil a real good hiding."

"Listen to that," said Till to his father. "And all I'm doing is riding along behind you, all quiet and as nice as can be."

Till's father didn't say anything, but just moved Till to sit in front of him.

On they rode, but now Till was more careful, keeping his face looking straight ahead so his father couldn't see how he stuck out his tongue, screwed up his mouth, twitched his nose and rolled his eyes round and round.

Again the people started shouting, "Did you ever see such a child? How dare you, you disgusting creature!"

Poor old Mr Owlyglass. He leant forward to Till and said, "Well, son, you must have been born unlucky. You're as quiet and as nice as can be and all the people yell horrible things at you. You don't deserve it, son."

"You see," said Till, "isn't that what I said? They're trouble-makers round here. Now you know what I have to put up with."

And Till's father believed him. He really did think that his son was getting unfair treatment. In fact he took it so badly that in the end he couldn't stand it any more, and he left home. He left Mrs Owlyglass all on her own with Till.

* * *

"What happened next?" said my brother.

Old Man Horst looked at the clock.

"Well now, boys, I think I've been talking long enough. You run along back to your room till dinner time, and if you think you want to hear any more about our friend Till Owlyglass, you come and see me tomorrow."

"When are you going to cure us of being bad?" said my brother.

"Aha," said Horst, "wait and see," and off we went.

THE SECOND DAY

WHEN WE HEAR HOW TILL OWLYGLASS
CAUSED TWO THIEVES TO FIGHT WITH
EACH OTHER, AND HOW HE REPAID A
MEAN FARMER WHO HAD FORCED HIM
TO EAT GREASY SOUP

The next day Mum and Dad went off to work
and my brother and me were left on our own
again. My brother wanted to play coal mining.
That's where one of us hid an apple in the bed
and the other had to find it.

But I said, "Let's go and see Old Man Horst and
hear another Till Owlglass story."

"It's Till Owlyglass," said my brother. "OK,
let's go," and off we went running downstairs to
his door.

"You knock."

"No, you knock."

"All right, I'll knock."

I knocked. There was the gruff voice again, asking who it was.

"It's us," I said.

"Come in," said Old Man Horst, and again we walked into the little dark room, and this time it seemed much more friendly than last time.

"Well," said Horst. "What can I do for you two boys today?"

My brother spoke first. "Can you tell us another Till Owlyglass story, please?"

"Well, sit down, sit down; and I'll see what I can remember," said Horst.

* * *

Till was getting older and sometimes he would spend whole nights away from home getting up to mischief. He'd be out stealing apples off neighbours' trees, letting dogs loose to chase the cats and goodness knows what else.

Once, after a night of this kind of fooling, he felt tired and thought he'd like to lie down and have a sleep. He was in one of the villagers' gardens at the time, a man who kept bees, and Till, who knew every nook and cranny of the village, knew which of this man's hives were full of bees and which were empty. The night was getting cold, so he climbed into one of the empty beehives, snuggled down to get warm and went to sleep.

Some time later Till woke up. He heard whispers right next to him. It was two men, thieves.

"Which one shall we have, then?" says one.

"The new one," says the other.

"No, no, no! The one we take has got to be the heaviest one."

"Why?"

"Why? Because the heaviest one will be the one with the most honey in it, won't it, eh? Use your brains, son."

"Right, yeah, I get it."

Then Till heard the two men going round the hives lifting them up, feeling which one was the heaviest. So, of course, you know what happened, don't you? They soon found out that the hive with Till inside it was the heaviest.

"This is the one, pal. Come on, let's go."

At once Till felt himself being lifted up into the air and carried along. He could just see each of the two men through cracks in the hive. While the fellow behind was looking round, up popped Till, grabbed the hair of the man in front and heaved. Then he quickly ducked back into the hive.

"Hey," said the man. "What do you think you're playing at? Leave off pulling my hair."

"What are you talking about?" said the other one. "I didn't pull your hair."

"Hmph!" said the first.

As soon as he could, Till popped up again and gave the same man another great tug of his hair.

"Now cut it out, will you," said the man. "Quit this fooling about or I'll drop the whole darned hive."

"Look," said the other. "I don't know what

29

you're talking about, but you're making enough racket to wake the whole village up. We'll get caught carrying this thing and then we really *will* be in trouble. So shut up, will you."

Till could scarcely stop himself from squealing with laughter.

A few more minutes passed and Till watched for his chance again. This time he went for the man behind. Up he popped and brought his hand down smack on top of the man's head. And, just as quickly, he popped back into the hive. The man was furious.

"You pig. What did you hit me for? I told you I wasn't pulling your hair." At that, he just dropped his side of the hive and slammed out at the man in front.

So then the man in front said, "Don't you hit me. First you pull my hair, then you lie about me hitting you. I've had enough." And he thumped the other chap right in the chest. Next thing, the two of them were rolling on the ground punching and thumping and biting and kicking. Little Till watched for a while, and then just as soon as he could, he was off and away across the fields back to his bed, where his mother found him in the morning, just as if nothing had happened.

* * *

"Is that the end of that one?" I said.

"Yes," Horst answered.

"Can we have another one?" said my brother.

Horst looked at the clock. "Well, I'm not sure about that, I have some things to do."

"Please," my brother said.

"Go on, just one."

"All right, all right. Let me think for a moment ..."

* * *

In the olden days there was a nice thing that

31

people did. Every so often a farmer invited all his neighbours' children over for a feast on the day after he had killed his pig. And in those days people used every single little bit of the pig – they ate the tail, the trotters and they made all kinds of sausages and pies and black pudding. The custom was that the children had the sausages and black pudding at the feast.

In Till's village there was a farmer who was a terrible miser. He was so mean that when his family had chicken for dinner, he'd sit the children on the floor and only give them the bones to chew.

Well, it was this farmer's turn to kill his pig and give a feast to all the children in Till's village. Of course, one thing he couldn't bear was the idea of giving all these children nice things to eat. So he invited them over, but instead of dishing up all the lovely little treats of sausages and black pudding, he ladled out bowlfuls of cold greasy soup, the kind of stuff that makes you feel sick just thinking about putting it into your mouth. And as if that wasn't bad enough, he cut big chunks of hard, mouldy bread and dropped them into this horrible greasy soup. No one wanted any of it, but this mean and horrible farmer stood behind the children with a big stick, forcing them to eat.

"Come on," he yelled. "You thought you'd have something for free, eh? Well, here it is. Eat up." And there, among all these children, was Till.

"Come on, Owlyglass," the man laughed and sneered. "Fill your face with it, son. Do you the world of good, it will."

Finally, after an hour or so of this torture, he let the children go, knowing that next year when he said he was going to have the feast, no one would come. And that was his plan.

The children all rushed home and were sick for the rest of the day or longer. Till was really angry, and he was old enough now to think that no one played a trick on him without getting a trick played back on them. And that's the way it was. Till plotted and schemed how to get back at the mean farmer.

In the end, what he did was take four pieces of bread and tie them together to make a cross. He slipped this into his pocket and strolled off to the mean farmer's chicken run. He climbed up on to the wall, and threw the cross among the chickens. The chickens fell on it, and soon they were tugging and heaving on the ends of the bread. But the ends were tied together, so the more they tugged, the nearer they got to one another, tugging and pulling and pecking and screeching. This went on and on, until four chickens flew up into a tree, still joined together by the bread.

The mean farmer heard the racket and came rushing out, thinking it was a fox. He saw all his chickens in a terrible state, losing feathers and fighting like mad; and four of them were all in a

tangle up the tree. He also saw Till sitting on the wall, grinning all over his face. There was nothing the farmer could do but cut those four chickens down and have them for supper that night. All the money he thought he had saved by not giving the children a proper feast he had now lost by having to eat those chickens. He cursed the children and he cursed Till. "Hell's bells! If I ever get my hands on you, Owlyglass, I'll have you skinned alive!"

But it was no good. He knew, and of course Till knew, that Till had got his own back. And Till went on sitting on the wall, out of reach of the mean old farmer, still grinning all over his face.

* * *

"That Till is wicked," said my brother.

"And so he was," said Old Man Horst.

"Can we have another one?" I said.

"Oh no," said Horst. "That's it for this morning. It's time you two went back for your dinner."

"Well," I said, "if you can't tell us another story, can you give us the cure for being bad? What is it? Medicine?"

Horst laughed. "Maybe next time. Just wait and see, little fellow," he said to me. "Now off you go."

And yes, off we went.

THE THIRD DAY

WHEN WE HEAR HOW TILL OWLYGLASS
FELL FROM A TIGHTROPE, AND HOW
HE PERSUADED A GREAT MANY PEOPLE
TO GIVE HIM THEIR SHOES

Next day I got to thinking about Till Owlyglass.
He seemed to be just about the worst person I'd
ever heard of. Even worse than me, I thought.

When my brother woke up, he said he'd been
dreaming that he'd met Till and they'd gone
off on a trip together and got up to all sorts of
wicked things.

So I said, "What things?"

And he said, "Aha, not saying," and that made
me really cross.

So I said, "Well, I'm going to see Horst on
my own today."

"No, you're not," said my brother. "We're both going."

And sure enough, as soon as we could, we slipped downstairs to see Old Man Horst.

"What do you want today?" said Horst.

"Another Owlyglass story, of course," said my brother.

"Oh," said Horst. "I thought you were coming for your medicine. The medicine to stop you being bad."

So I said, "Tell us a story first and then give us the medicine."

"All right," said Horst, "if that's the way you want it ..."

* * *

Till was living with his mother, who was very, very poor; and as soon as Till was old enough, his mother wanted him to learn a trade so that he could earn some money to help them live.

"Why don't you become a tailor?" she said.

"Oh no," said Till. "Locked up all day, bending over a needle and thread – I couldn't do that, I'd go blind."

"Why don't you become a baker, then?"

"Oh no," said Till. "Standing next to an oven all day, heaving loaves of bread in and out – I couldn't do that, I'd get roasted alive."

"Why don't you become a miller, then?" she said.

"Oh no," said Till. "Stuck in a windmill, breathing in all the flour dust – I couldn't do that, I'd choke to death."

Till found fault with everything his mother suggested because he didn't want to work. He just wanted to loaf about, day in, day out.

In the Owlyglass house there was a loft up in the roof, where nobody went. Do you know what Till did up there? He stretched a rope from one corner of the room to the other, and whenever he could, he went up there and practised walking on the rope. Day after day he practised until finally he could do it.

So one day he took his rope and instead of tying it up inside the loft, he tied one end of it to the window and from there he took it across the village stream (where he'd tumbled on the day he was baptised) and tied it to a tree on the other side.

Then he stepped out of the window on to the rope and stood there whistling.

Soon the whole village came out to watch him.

"Hey, come over here, look, it's Owlyglass! Look what he's up to now." "He can't do that. He'll fall." "You never know with that clown. He may not do a stroke of work but there are some things he's good at." "Yes, causing trouble mostly."

The children were there, cheering Till on. "Come on, Till. Walk, walk, walk!"

So off went Till. "First, ladies and gentlemen, the Walk. Watch closely. See that my feet never leave my legs." He walked the rope. "And now,

the Sit," and he sat on the rope. Then he did a
little dance and the crowd loved it. Even people
who hated him were saying, "Well, I suppose
he's got the knack, the little devil."

Till was feeling so pleased with himself

that he didn't notice his mother creep into the room where the rope was tied. Just as he was saying, "Ladies and gentlemen, men, women and children, I will now perform the famous Owlyglass Cartwheel," Mrs Owlyglass cut the rope and down Till tumbled, straight into the stream.

Everyone cheered. Mrs Owlyglass shouted down at Till, "That'll teach you a lesson, son. If you can't be bothered to go out and earn a decent penny to help your poor old mother, don't waste everyone's time with your stupid tricks."

Till climbed out of the stream, covered in mud and slime. Everyone was laughing and jeering at him.

"Lovely cartwheel, Till. Ho ho ho! Great Till, the tightrope walker!"

"That was his downfall, wasn't it?" said the village baker.

All the children came up to him, pointing and grinning and calling him names. "Till Muddyglass! Muddypants! Muddypants!"

In the end, Till crept back indoors feeling very sorry for himself. His mother certainly got the better of him that time.

* * *

"But did he get his own back, like with the man and the greasy soup?" I asked.

"Well, maybe he did, maybe he didn't," said Horst. "But you don't want me to tell you that one now, do you?"

"Yes, yes, yes," we went. "Come on, Horst."

* * *

A few days later Till took his rope out again. This time he tied one end to the church tower and the other to the village hall, right across the market place.

"Ladies and gentlemen," said Till, stepping out

on to the rope. "The Great Owlyglass will now perform a completely new set of tricks for you."

Of course the people all came running up, but now they called out, "Going for a swim are you, Till? Try diving into the market place!" "Is that Till or a fish up there?" and so on.

Till ignored them. "Ladies and gentlemen," he went on, "here, in its full glory, is the Cartwheel you were so unlucky not to see last week." And he turned a cartwheel. "And now, ladies and gentlemen, the Great Owlyglass doesn't just walk on his feet like other mortals, here he walks on his hands." And off he went on his hands down the rope. People were impressed. No question of it, they were amazed, and soon he'd won them over once again. They were clapping after every trick he did.

At last Till stopped and sat down on the rope and made a special announcement. "Ladies and gentlemen, I now come to the highlight of my performance. I will perform for you one of the most daring and amazing tricks ever seen in the whole history of tightrope walking. I shall need your help to perform this incredible trick. I must ask you, ladies and gentlemen, to lend me your shoes. The more you can let me have, the better the show will be. If you'd be so kind, just throw me up your shoes one by one, and you will see the most sensational trick in the world."

Soon all the people were throwing their shoes in the air, wondering just what Till was going to do with them.

As Till caught the shoes, he tied them together with a long piece of string. Up they came: slippers, boots, children's shoes, clogs, everything. And all the time, Till kept talking. "Lovely pair of shoes, madam. I'm sure they go round a lovely pair of feet. Thank you, sir, a nice boot, I wouldn't like

that up my backside on a dark night," and so on.

Finally Till had nearly a hundred shoes tied together. "Ladies and gentlemen, I will now

perform the trick. Watch closely. Feast your eyes on this fantastic display of skill."

Till swung the shoes once round his head, twice, three times, until they were whirring round at quite a pace. Then suddenly he let go and the shoes sailed across the market place and they landed on the street some way off.

Till bowed. "Thank you so much for helping me, ladies and gentlemen. You may have your shoes back."

So off everyone went to collect their shoes.

Soon there was a great heap of people, tugging and pulling at the knots and at one another, and arguing over whose shoe was whose. Till sat on the rope and watched it all.

"That's my boot!" "Get off!" "That's my wife's slipper, you fool!" "Don't you call me a fool!"

One by one people found their shoes, and began to realise it was all another of Till's tricks. They turned round, ready to tear him limb from limb, but he'd slipped off his rope and sneaked away from the village. And he thought it was a good idea to stay away for a few days until things had quietened down.

* * *

"Those people were just like the chickens in the other story," said my brother.

"Maybe he learnt how to play that trick by seeing what happened to the chickens," Horst said.

"He couldn't have known that the people

would behave just like a load of hens, could he?"

"He found out in the end, didn't he?"

"Hey," I said, looking at the clock. "It's dinner time. Sorry, we've got to go now, Horst. Bye." And off we went.

Half-way through dinner I remembered we hadn't asked about the medicine to stop us being bad. But there was plenty of time for that another day, I thought.

THE FOURTH DAY

WHEN WE HEAR HOW TILL OWLYGLASS
SOLD FLEA POWDER AND ACQUIRED
A WONDER HORSE, AND HOW HE
ADVERTISED THAT HE WOULD FLY OVER
MAGDEBURG MARKET SQUARE

The next day I decided it was time to ask Old Man Horst to give us the medicine to stop us from being bad. I told my brother we must ask Horst about it just as soon as we got in to see him.

So, when it was time to slip downstairs to Horst's room, we were ready to go right in and ask him for it. We arrived at his door, knocked and went in. But Horst was the first to speak.

"Ah, boys, I've been thinking about you.

Today is a special day for our stories."

"What do you mean?" I said.

"Till leaves home," said Horst.

"Why?" said my brother.

"Because his mother throws him out. It was not like nowadays, you know. You see his mother tried and tried to get Till to learn something, any ordinary way to earn a living. But no matter what she did, all he seemed to do was play the fool, learn silly tricks, or lie about all day dreaming of the great places he'd like to visit."

So Horst began the story, and we never had the medicine.

* * *

Sometimes Till just sat at home practising funny faces, screwing up his eyes, poking out his tongue and twisting up his nose. Sometimes he practised great speeches he'd make if he met a king or queen. Sometimes he'd pretend to be a great doctor or a great scholar, and practise speaking like them.

One day, Till was in the middle of one of his speeches. "I am the great Till Owlyglass, one of the world's most famous builders. I drew up the plans for the great cathedral in Paris. I showed the King of Denmark how to build his palace."

And suddenly there was his mother with, "Till Owlyglass, I've had just about as much as I can take. You sit here, day in, day out, doing nothing to pay your way. I slave away all day to get us enough bread to eat and you, a strong young man, spend your days talking to yourself in fancy talk and doing the most stupid things anyone has ever seen. I can't stand it any more, Till. I've got only one thing to say to you. Get out."

A year or so earlier, Till might have argued, "Oh, Mother, tomorrow I'll get down to it. I'm going to learn how to be a butcher. I've bought

a knife and an apron and I'm starting tomorrow."
And his mother would have believed him.

But today Till was different. He was beginning
to feel like a big fish in a little pond, a person
who was only famous in his own small village.
He thought it was time he went out into
the world.

"Mother," said Till, putting on one of his voices,
"I can see I have made your heart sore. Fear not, I
shall go forth into the world to seek my fortune."

"Oh, stop your silly talk," said Mrs Owlyglass.
"Just go, and don't bother me for the moment.
I can't stand it any more."

So, with no more fuss, Till put on his shoes and
walked out of the door, never to return again.

Till knew where he was going. He headed
for Magdeburg, a town with a big market, a big
town, not just a little place like Kneitlingen.

After a few days he arrived there and at once

began to mingle with the crowd in the market, watching the buying and selling, listening to the shouting, studying the street performers. He loved it, and pretty soon he thought that he could do as well as any of the people he saw there. There were people selling chickens that couldn't lay eggs, people juggling and dropping their clubs, people selling pills to stop your hair falling out. Till watched it all. And then he made his plans. He didn't have a penny in his pocket. What could he do? Well, what he did was collect together a little ash from an old rubbish dump, and he mixed it with a little dust from a stone wall.

Next, he took the mixture and shook it into some old nut shells.

And then, when he had made up a whole pile of these, he went back to the market, found himself a little corner, spread his nutshells full of the mixture out in front of him and began to shout.

"Step forward, ladies and gentlemen. Before you, you see a powder. Madam, I can see you standing there, scratching your arm. Perhaps you wonder why. I can tell you. Fleas! Yes, fleas,

madam, nothing to be ashamed of, this town is full of them. Sir, I see you scratching your backside. It's fleas. I, the famous Till Owlyglass, can put an end to all your itching and scratching. Here, before your very eyes, you see the amazing Owlyglass flea powder. All you need is my famous powder and it'll be no more itching, no more scratching."

By now people had begun to gather round. They were interested in Till's speechifying and they wanted to get a close look at those little nutshells full of powder.

"I can see you're interested, madam. As you're the first, please take one for free. I'm an honest man, madam. Take a nutshell of powder and it'll be no more itching, no more scratching for you."

Soon crowds of people were asking Till if they could have one.

"Of course, sir. Of course, madam. They're on

special offer today, half price to the people of Magdeburg. Two shillings. No more itching, no more scratching."

In the space of twenty minutes, Till sold every one of his nutshells full of ash and dust. With the money jingling in his pouch, he went off to the nearest inn and made his plans.

After he had drunk a bit and eaten a bit he went off to the knacker's yard – the place where they kill old horses that are too weak to work any more. There he bought himself the cheapest horse he could.

Then Till led this poor old horse behind a wall on the edge of the market and tied its tail to a post. Once again he began his speechifying.

"Walk up, walk up, and take a look! Ladies and gentlemen, on the other side of this wall you can feast your eyes on a rare and remarkable sight. Come and look at the Wonder Horse. Its head is where its tail should be. Do not miss this chance to see an extraordinary freak of nature. Pay your money and take a look."

Many people couldn't resist Till's offer. They thought, This sounds interesting, let's take a look. They paid their money, and Till helped them over the wall. Of course, what they saw

was just an ordinary old horse with its tail tied to a post. And when they came back among their friends, they didn't tell them it was a trick, because they wanted their friends to be tricked as well. So one person after another climbed over the wall, and all the time Till was taking their money.

But after a while Till's luck ran out. One of the ladies who had bought his ash and dust the day before, the world-famous Owlyglass flea powder, came along, and she was on to him straightaway. "It's you, you rogue. You're a liar and a cheat. That stuff you sold me yesterday was no use at all. I saw a flea walk all over it. You robbed me of good money with that rubbish."

"Madam, madam, madam," said Till. "Perhaps you didn't understand me right. That flea powder has to be used in a special way. You should take a needle or a pin, put the flea onto the end of the pin, then pinch the flea between your finger and thumb, to make its jaws open. Then you put some of my powder on the end of a tiny stick and ram it down its throat. As soon as one grain touches its tongue the flea is dead, as dead as a doornail, madam."

The woman listened to all this. Then she said, "What are you talking about, you fool? If I had the time to do all that, I might just as well have pinched the flea with my nail in the first place, and killed it like that."

All this time people were crowding round, some who had been tricked by the Wonder Horse, and others who had been tricked by the flea powder. Till could see that they were beginning to get angry.

"The man's a fool, and we've been tricked." "Huh! He thought he'd come to this place and get the better of us, did he?" "If there's one thing I can't abide, it's a plain out and out fool."

Till thought the best thing he could do was disappear for a bit. Without hanging about any more, he hopped over the wall, ran down the alley and round the corner, and went straight to an inn on the edge of town.

* * *

Old Man Horst stopped there.

"I suppose that's all for today, is it?" I said.

"Well, actually, no. I haven't finished with Till in Magdeburg, I was just giving myself a break," said Horst.

"Oh, go on then," we said.

* * *

The thing is, Till was a bit cross with himself that the crowd had got the better of him, and he hadn't liked the way they called him a fool. So after a day or two of thinking, he came out on the streets again, this time wrapped in an old cloak.

"Ladies and gentlemen, today the great Till Owlyglass will fly like a bird over the market square."

He went all over the town calling this out, telling the people to come to the Town Hall at two o'clock.

By two o'clock nearly the whole town was standing in front of the Town Hall, and exactly as the clock struck, Till stepped out on to the roof.

There was a hush, as hundreds and hundreds of people looked up. Till began to flap his arms, first slowly, then faster and faster. The people down below began to whisper and get excited. "He's going to take off any moment now," they were saying.

Suddenly Till stopped and burst out laughing. He pointed at them and shouted, "Well, well, well, friends! Up to now, I believed I was the biggest fool around. Many people told me so, even some of you. But now I see you are all much bigger fools than me. How do I know this? Well, great fool I may be, but never for one moment would I have believed that Till Owlyglass could fly. After all, you can see I'm not a bird, I'm not a bat, I'm not a butterfly. I would never have believed that I could step from the top of this huge Town Hall without falling to the ground and breaking my neck. But you, you

actually believed I could fly. And so, ladies and gentlemen, I tell you that you are all bigger fools than me. I think I have proved it, don't you?"

At that, he turned round and disappeared.

The people stood speechless. Till was right. There was no getting away from it. Some of them shrugged their shoulders, some of them laughed, some of them nudged one another and giggled, but they all knew that he was right.

Till, meanwhile, ran as fast as his legs could carry him away from Magdeburg. He thought that the best thing for him to do was not to be seen there much more, in case the people's laughter turned to anger. Because if that happened, they'd skin him alive.

* * *

"And that is really all for today, boys," said Horst. "Off you go. I've been talking much too long already."

"Ask him about the medicine," said my brother.

"No, you ask him about the medicine."

But Old Man Horst got us out of the door and closed it behind us before either of us could say another word.

THE FIFTH DAY

WHEN WE HEAR HOW TILL OWLYGLASS
MADE A LOT OF MONEY OUT OF HIS
HAT, AND HOW HE BAKED OWLS
AND MONKEYS

The next day my brother said he wanted to spend all day in bed.

I said, "You can't do that, you'll go mouldy."

And he said, "I'm fed up with this holiday in Germany, I'm just going to spend all day in bed."

So I said, "Maybe we ought to go and ask Old Man Horst for some medicine to stop us being bored."

"Yes," said my brother, and he jumped out of bed and he had all his clothes on, even his shoes. He'd got dressed while I was still asleep.

"How's that for an Owlyglass trick?" he said.

"Well, come on," I said. "Let's go and ask Old Man Horst for some medicine to stop us being bored."

So after breakfast, and after Mum and Dad had gone off to do their work, we went down to Old Man Horst. The first thing we said to him was, "Have you got any medicine to stop us being bored?"

And he said, "Well, boys, we haven't sorted out your medicine for being bad yet."

"Well, which one shall we have first?" I said.

"Maybe you should have both at the same time," said Horst.

"Right," we said.

"Well, I'll see what I can do," said Horst. "Now, are you having an Owlyglass story today, or what?"

"Owlyglass story, please."

"Right," said Horst.

* * *

Till Owlyglass was running away from Magdeburg and heading for Brandenburg, and all the money he had left was four shillings. As he walked along the road he came to an inn. There he sat down and watched to see what would happen. He hadn't sat there long when two soldiers came by. He knew that they were officers and so their pockets would be full of money. They saw Till sitting there in his country-style hat and started to laugh at him.

So Till said, "You think my hat's funny, do you? Well, I can show you that this hat's not just any old hat. This hat's worth a lot of money, you know. If you don't believe me, come into this inn and have a meal with me."

The soldiers thought they had nothing to lose and said, "Right, you'll pay, will you?"

"Oh, don't worry about that," said Till.

And all three went inside to eat.

The two soldiers sat down, and Till went over and had a quick chat with the landlady, and gave her the four shillings.

The dinner was served and it was excellent – soup, beef and roast potatoes, lovely pies and puddings, and plenty to drink. The two soldiers sat there laughing and smacking their lips, saying, "Lovely meal, lovely meal."

When they had finished, Till called the landlady over and said, "How much money do you want for the meal?"

And the landlady said, "Four shillings."

At that, Till took off his hat and turned it round four times on the end of his finger.

"Thank you, sir," said the landlady, and went back to her business. Of course, Till had given her the four shillings before, hadn't he?

The officers were amazed. "Staggering! What

a wonderful hat! You've got an incredible hat there, old boy," they said.

"Ah well," said Till, "there you have it, lads. Now you see what I mean when I said this hat's worth a lot. I tell you, if I had all the money that people have said they'd give me for this hat, I'd be a rich man today."

So one of the soldiers said, "If I offered you

some money, would you sell your hat? With a hat like yours we'd never go hungry, would we?"

So Till said he might and he might not and he pretended he wasn't really interested, so as to make the two soldiers offer even more money. But in the end he said, "All right, all right," and he sold them the hat for forty shillings.

The next day the soldiers came back to the inn with a big group of their friends and ordered a huge banquet. Till hid in a cupboard to watch what was going on. The dinner went on and on for ages. At the end one of the soldiers asked the landlady, "How much?"

"Eight shillings," said the landlady, so the soldier started turning the hat round and round and round.

"Eight shillings, I said," said the landlady, and the soldier went on turning the hat round and round.

The landlady got cross. "I don't know what you think you're doing, twiddling your silly hat round and round. I want my money. If you don't pay up, I'll have you arrested."

There was nothing for it, the fellow had to pay up. And everyone sat there mocking him and turning their hats round and round and laughing their heads off.

The two soldiers left the inn in a fury. "If I see that fellow who sold us that hat, I'll have him arrested, put in chains and flung into prison."

Till sat still in the cupboard, grinning all over his face.

* * *

So I said to Horst, "Did they catch him?"

"You wait and see," said Horst, and he went straight on with the story.

* * *

In time Till travelled on to Brandenburg, where he spent all his money on food and drink and having a good time, until in the end the money ran out. So he had to think of something else to do.

One person he had met in Brandenburg was a master baker, a big rich man who was always boasting, saying, "I am the biggest and the best baker around."

When Till met him one day in the market square, he said, "I hear you are looking for someone to help you in the bakery. I'm a baker from a village on the other side of Germany. Can I do the job?"

The man looked Till up and down and said, "Right, I'll take you on."

"Where is your shop, sir?" said Till.

"Over there," said the baker. "You see where that window goes right down to the ground? Go right in there and present yourself to my wife."

So Till strode across the market square. When he got to the window he just walked straight into it, smashed it to pieces and went on into the shop.

The baker's wife was there. "What's going on?" she yelled. "What do you think you're doing? You've just smashed our best window. What are you? Some kind of idiot?"

"Madam," said Till, "I have only done as I was told. Your husband, the master baker, told me to walk into your shop just where the window goes down to the ground. So I did."

Of course the woman couldn't say anything to that.

A few minutes later the master baker himself came in. "What the devil's going on here?" he roared.

"Ah, master," said Till. "I'm glad you've come. You can explain to your wife how you told me to walk into your shop just where the window goes down to the ground. I've done just as you told me, haven't I, sir? That's all I want, to do exactly what you tell me to do, sir."

At first the master baker was furious, but then he thought, Perhaps I've got a really good man here, a man who does exactly as he's told. So he decided to keep Till on. After all, he might make more money out of someone like this.

"Now then," said the man. "I want you to watch the shop for now, and tonight I want you to get on with the baking. Do you under-stand me?"

"Of course," said Till. "What do you want me to bake?"

The master baker looked amazed. "What do I want you to bake? You're a baker and you don't know what to bake! What do you think? I want you to bake Owls and monkeys? Now get down to it, son. I'll have a shopful of customers in the morning."

That night Till went downstairs to bake, and the master baker went to bed. But Till didn't bake bread and rolls, which is what the master baker really wanted. He shaped the dough into little bread owls and little bread monkeys and baked them. When it was all finished there were rows and rows of owls and monkeys. The shop was full of them.

In the morning the master baker came down and the first thing he saw was all those owls and monkeys. He flew into a rage. "What have you done? Are you crazy or something? You'll ruin my business. All the housewives will be here soon to get their bread and all I'll have for them is this. First you smash my front window and now you bake this nonsense. What in heaven's name made you do it?"

"Well, master," said Till. "What you said was, 'What do you think I want you to bake? Owls and monkeys?' so I only did as I was told."

"Oh, you know very well I didn't mean that, you great lump of an idiot you! Now just get yourself and your backside out of here, and you can take your infernal owls and monkeys with you, for all I care. I've got to close the shop today, thanks to you. One broken window and no bread. What a day! What a day!"

So Till calmly collected up all the little bread owls and monkeys and took them off to the market.

There he set himself up and called out, "Owls and monkeys! Funny bread, funny bread! Come and buy, come and buy!" And what do you know – people laughed at Till's funny bread,

and children begged their mums and dads to buy them funny bread. Soon Till was selling away like mad. And when the master baker looked out of his shop and saw Till selling owls and monkeys, there was nothing he could do. Because hadn't he told Till to clear out of his shop taking all his owls and monkeys with him? Wasn't Till doing just what he'd been told?

* * *

"How much money did Till make that day?" said my brother.

"I'm not absolutely sure," said Horst. "I don't remember exactly, but I know he did very well for himself. But then, on the other hand, he knew he couldn't stay in Brandenburg very long, or both the soldiers and the master baker would be on his tail."

Just then I heard my dad calling.

"Aha," said Horst, "that's your dad on your tails. You'd better go and see what he wants." And so both of us were out the door in a flash.

THE SIXTH DAY

WHEN WE HEAR HOW TILL OWLYGLASS
HAD HIS BOOTS GREASED ALL OVER,
HOW HE SEWED INVISIBLE STITCHES
AND HOW HE TOLD A GREAT SECRET
TO THE TAILORS OF SAXONY

The next day, when I got up, I said to my brother, "Look, I don't feel like hearing a story today, let's muck about like we used to."

"No, no," said my brother. "I want to hear some more stories."

"No, no," I said. "I want to play about. You remember that time we did theatres from behind the curtain?"

"Yes, I do remember," said my brother. "You pulled down the curtain. Look, I want to hear some more stories. If you want to muck about

84

in here on your own, you can."

"Look," I said. "I can't play football on my own, can I?"

"Well, you'll have to come with me then, won't you?"

So off we went to see Horst again.

As soon as we got in, my brother said, "He didn't want to come today, he wanted to muck about."

So that made me look stupid. And Horst could see that, so he said to my brother, "Leave him alone. Perhaps he'll change his mind when he hears what Till did next."

* * *

Till was in Leipzig, and by now people all over Germany were beginning to talk about him. The bakers told the butchers, and the butchers told the tailors, and the tailors told the landladies, and the landladies told the barrel-makers, and they all said the same thing, "Look out for Till Owlyglass, he may trick you."

One day Till went to the shoe-mender to have his boots greased – in the old days people used to put grease on their boots to keep them soft. Till was just saying, "I'll have my boots greased all over, please," when the young boy in the shop, the apprentice, recognised him. He rushed over to his master and whispered, "Do you know who this is, master? This is Till Owlyglass, the famous trickster. We must do exactly as he says or he'll do something awful to us."

"You're quite right, son," said the shoe-mender. "Do as you're told. Grease his boots really well so he can't complain about a thing."

But as soon as the boy got down to work, he remembered the story he had heard about Till baking owls and monkeys, and doing just as he was told, and he thought, I could do that! Till asked me to have his boots greased all over, and that's what I'll do. And he set to greasing the boots all over, inside and out.

A few days later Till came to collect his boots.

"Here they are," said the shoe-mender. "I hope you're satisfied, sir."

Till saw what the boy had done, so he laughed and said, "Oh, very good. You're a clever fellow, aren't you? No one has ever greased my boots so well before. Greased all over. Exactly. Well, well, I like to see people doing what I ask them to do. How much do I owe you?"

"That'll be two shillings, sir," said the shoe-mender, so Till paid, and off he went.

The boy then told his master what he had done and they both had a good laugh over it, saying, "For once Till Owlyglass has had a dose of his own medicine."

But Till was standing outside the shop window

listening to them, and without any warning, he put his head through the glass so that it broke into a thousand pieces and said, "I forgot to ask you, sir, what kind of grease did you use on my boots?"

The shoe-mender looked up. "What are you up to, you thug? You've just smashed my window."

"Don't let it get you down, master," Till said.

"I was only asking a polite question. What did you grease my boots with?"

The shoe-mender was too annoyed to answer, so Till pulled his head back and went off whistling happily.

But not before he heard the master yelling at the boy. "This is all your fault, son, and you'll have to pay for it. You thought you'd get even with Till Owlyglass, did you? Now who's the biggest fool, eh? He can easily go off somewhere and clean his shoes, but I can't stick my window together, can I? He's tricked me just like he did the master baker in Brandenburg. I shall make you pay for this, don't you worry. It'll teach you one lesson – better that we suffer Owlyglass than try to beat him at his own game."

* * *

"And that's the end of that one," said Horst.

My brother said, "Did Till ever do any more of

that business of doing just as he was told?"

"Yes, he did," said Horst. "I'll tell you about it next."

* * *

One time Till went to a tailor and said, "I'm a tailor and I'm looking for work."

And the tailor said, "Good, I need someone to help me."

"What do you want me to do?" said Till.

"Well," said the tailor, "I want you to do some sewing that can't be seen by anyone. Can you do that?"

"Yes, of course," said Till.

So the tailor handed Till two pieces of cloth to be sewn together so well that the stitches could not be seen. And off he went. Till took the work and crept into a big box that happened to be sitting in the shop. There, in the pitch dark, he began sewing.

Some time later the tailor came back. He couldn't see Till, so he shouted out, "Hey, where are you?"

"I'm in here, master," said Till from inside the box.

"What are you doing there?" said the tailor.

And you know what Till said, don't you? He said, "I'm doing what you told me, master. You told me to do sewing that no one could see, so that's what I'm doing, aren't I? You can't see me sewing, can you?"

The tailor realised he had a fool on his hands, so he grabbed hold of Till by the scruff of his neck and booted him out of the shop. "Get out of here!" he said.

"What about my pay?" said Till.

"You ought to pay *me*," said the tailor, "for the material you've spoiled."

So Till was back on the streets, and he still had no money in his pockets.

After that Till thought he'd like to get his own back on tailors. He sent a letter to all the master tailors of Saxony and asked them to come and see him in the old town of Rostock. In the letter, he said he was going to tell them a secret which would help them and their children so much that they'd be rich and successful until the end of their days.

As soon as all the tailors received their letters they had meetings with one another to help them make up their minds what to do. They all decided that they wouldn't go. They said that would teach Till a lesson – he'd look a right fool having a meeting with no one at Rostock.

But secretly each tailor thought to himself, What if he really does have something to tell us? If I went, I could learn something that would help me do better than the next man, and I'd get more business, and I'd get richer and more successful...

So on the day, at Rostock, the town was jam-packed full of tailors, all come to hear what Till had to say. Till wandered about on his own, letting himself be seen and soon rich master tailors were approaching him and offering big sums of money for his secret.

But Till wouldn't have any of it. He said, "Come to the field outside the city wall tomorrow at three. There I will tell my secret to anyone who pays one shilling."

Well, of course many of the tailors had come a long way to hear what Till had to say, and to learn the secret that would help them so much. So they were quite happy to pay. And the next day, a great many of them came to the field outside the city wall, and also a great many other people who knew that something funny was bound to happen whenever Till was around.

The place was packed by the time Till stepped up on to a platform in the middle of the field. In front of him was a sea of faces stretching as far as he could see. And nearby was a barrel full of the shillings he'd collected.

Till made a low bow and began his speech.

"Good afternoon and welcome, honourable tailors. I'm glad you have realised that today's your chance to learn something for your own good. I see that many of you have come from a long way off. Now listen very carefully to what I say, so that you don't miss a single word."

"I guess most of you have got a pair of scissors, a tape-measure, a thimble, needles, thread and an iron. If you've got all that, then you've got the tools of your trade."

The tailors looked at one another.

"Well, you know all that of course, but what I'm going to tell you now, you must take note of and remember, because it is very, very important. Are you ready?"

They nodded.

"After you have threaded your needle, before you begin to sew, you must remember – are you listening? – you must remember to make a knot at the end of the thread. This will stop you sewing a line of stitches and then the thread falling out. In this way you will save many hours of time and work. You will become happy and rich.

"This is a great secret I am telling you. I am sure you will want to thank me for it, and you will think of me every time you sit down to sew."

Till made another low bow.

The tailors stood and looked at one another. Someone called out, "Everyone knows you have to tie a knot in the end of the thread. We've known that in our trade for thousands of years."

"Aha," said Till. "Then you ought to thank me for telling you the truth. But if you don't want to, I won't lose any sleep over it. You can all go home now, I won't keep you any more."

After that the tailors just wanted to get at Till with their scissors and irons. But he was off and away in no time at all, with his barrel of money under his arm. He knew how to lose himself among the townspeople who weren't tailors, who were all laughing their heads off at his trick. Up and down the field people were chanting, "Don't forget to tie a knot, don't forget to tie a knot." And Till wasn't seen round that way for a long time, I can tell you.

* * *

"Well," said Horst, "that's it. Look, can one of you get me a drink of water?"

"Yes," said my brother, and he got Horst a glass of water.

Just before Horst began to drink, my brother said, "Hang on a moment, Horst. I must just tell you a secret about drinking water. It really makes it taste much better."

"What's that?" said Horst.

"Remember to open your mouth before you

tip the water in, otherwise all the water spills down your front."

Horst laughed. "Oho, you think you're Till Owlyglass, do you? Now get out of here before I think up some trick to play on *you*."

Once again we were out of the room in a flash.

THE SEVENTH DAY

WHEN WE HEAR HOW TILL OWLYGLASS
CURED ALL THE PATIENTS IN
LUNEBURG HOSPITAL IN ONE DAY,
AND HOW HE RODE INTO LUNEBURG
ON A CARTFUL OF EARTH

The next day my brother said, "We've been going to see Old Man Horst for about a week now and you know we've never taken him anything."

"What do you mean?" I said.

"You know, a present or something, to say thank you for telling us all those stories."

"Well," I said, "I don't know what to take him."

"We could do a drawing," he said. "We could each choose a thing that Owlyglass did and do a drawing of it."

So that's what we did. We sat down and did

two big pictures of Owlyglass. I did one of Owlyglass on the tightrope and my brother did one of Owlyglass poking his head through the shoe-mender's window, and then we took them down with us to Horst.

"You're a bit late today, aren't you, lads?" said Horst. So my brother said it was because we were busy doing something, and we handed over the pictures.

I couldn't tell whether he was pleased or not. He just looked at them for a long time and then he put them on the table beside him. Then he picked them up again and said, "You haven't put your names on them, boys."

So we very carefully put our names on the bottom and my brother said, "We wrote something on the back as well."

So Horst turned the pictures over and he saw that we had each written, "Thank you

Horst for the Owlyglass stories."

"Now then, you two," he said, "I haven't been able to get hold of your medicine yet, but while I was looking I remembered the time Till had to do some curing. Do you want to hear this one?"

"We're ready for it," said my brother.

* * *

One day Till arrived in the city of Luneburg. This time he thought he'd try his luck at being a doctor, so he practised talking and behaving like a doctor. And then he put up notices on all the church doors saying that he could cure every kind of illness that anyone ever had.

"No matter what you've got wrong with you," Till said, "I can make you better."

Of course he didn't know how to do any such thing, but people believed him and people came to see him. And when they came to see Till, he would look at their tongues, and feel their heads, and ask them questions. Then he would look really serious and say, "Um, ah, yes ... I think you need a strong dose of warm water," and then the person would go away and drink warm water.

Sometimes they got better, perhaps because of the warm water, perhaps because they were going to get better anyway, or perhaps just because they believed that Till was a great doctor.

One day the man who was in charge of the town hospital came to see Till. "I hear that you are a great and wonderful doctor," he said, "and you can cure all illnesses. My hospital is very full at the moment, too full in fact. Do you think you could come and help me?"

So Till said, "Look, if I can cure all your patients in one day, so that there is nobody left in your hospital, will you give me two hundred pieces of gold?"

"If you can do it," said the man, "you can have the money."

"Right," said Till, "but first I'll have to go and see your patients to see what I've got to do to make them better."

The next day Till went off to the hospital, and there he walked from bed to bed looking at each patient. He also had something to say to each patient. He went and whispered in each patient's ear, "I want to tell you a secret, but you mustn't tell anyone else. You're very ill, but I know how to cure you. I want to give you back your health and strength, but to do this, I've got to take one of you, whoever is the *most* ill, and I've got to burn this really ill person down to powder. Then I'll mix the powder into a drink, give you the drink, and when you've drunk it you'll be better. I'm going to take the one who is the *most* ill to turn into powder, all right?"

Till told each patient that this was what he was going to do.

The next morning Till told the man in charge of the hospital that he had cured everybody.

"I can't believe it," said the man.

"Well," said Till, "all you have to do is stand at the door of your hospital and say that if any patients are feeling better, they can pack their bags and go."

So that's what the man did. He stood in the hospital doorway and called out, "All of you who are feeling better, take up your bags and go."

Well, you can guess what happened. All the patients were so afraid of being told they were the most ill and would be turned into powder and fed to the others that they got up out of bed and rushed out the door as fast as their legs would carry them.

The man in charge could scarcely believe

his eyes. "All better? So soon?" he said.

Then he went to the hospital treasury and gave Till two hundred pieces of gold.

A few days later some of the sick people started coming back.

"What's the matter?" said the man in charge. "Didn't I hire a famous doctor to make you all better? Why have you come back?"

When they told him what Till had said to them, he realised he had been tricked. But the two hundred pieces of gold were gone and there was nothing he could do about it. Then he thought to himself, Well, well, well, Owlyglass didn't do any worse than plenty of real doctors I have heard of, who couldn't cure anybody either.

The Duke of Luneburg, on the other hand, wasn't happy about it at all. It was his hospital, and Till's two hundred pieces of gold came out of his hospital funds. So he put up a notice saying that Till Owlyglass must never ever come again to Luneburg. He must never set foot in the Duke of Luneburg's town or on any of the Duke of Luneburg's land. If he did he would be put to death.

When Till heard about this, he couldn't stop himself from thinking up a way in which he could get back to Luneburg and not be put to death. But how could he do it?

Well, he had an idea. He saw a farmer carting cow manure and putting it on his field and he went up to the farmer and asked, "Who does this land belong to?"

"It's mine," said the farmer. "I inherited it from my father and he had it from his."

"Good," said Till. "Now, if I put some of your land in a cart, how much would it cost me?"

The farmer thought a bit and said, "A shilling."

So Till said, "Fine."

Till went off, bought himself a horse and cart, came back to the farmer, loaded up the cart with some earth from the farmer's land, and paid the farmer his shilling. Then he sat on top of the earth and set out for Luneburg.

As soon as Till arrived on the Duke of Luneburg's land, he was recognised and people began shouting, "That's him, that's the man who tricked us. That's Till Owlyglass." And when the Duke of Luneburg himself caught sight of Till out of his carriage window, he ordered the coachman to drive up to Till and he shouted out

of the window, "Didn't I tell you never to set foot on my land ever again? Right, you will die. You will be hanged today from the town gallows."

"Ah, master, stop there," said Till. "You know how I always do as I'm told. But, sir, I'm not on your land, I'm on my land. A man's got the right to be on his own land, hasn't he? The land I'm sitting on I bought off a farmer this morning. I know it's mine. I'm on my own land here, sir," and he pointed at the earth he was sitting on.

The Duke couldn't stop himself from laughing. "All right, Owlyglass. I'll let you go this time. But take your land off my land as fast as you can, and don't you ever let me see you again, because if I do, I'll have you and your horse and cart put to death at once."

So Till turned the cart round, and waving to

the crowd and still sitting on his land, he rode out of town.

* * *

"That was a close one," I said. "He nearly got caught that time."

"You wait till next time, then," said Horst.

"Does he get caught next time?" I said.

"You wait and see."

"Will you have the medicine for us next time?" said my brother.

"Well," said Horst, "what I have to do is grind one of you ..."

"Quick," I said, "Let's get out of here."

And off we went.

THE EIGHTH DAY

WHEN WE HEAR HOW
TILL OWLYGLASS STOLE A JUG OF WINE
IN LUBECK, AND HOW HE USED GREAT
CUNNING TO ESCAPE BEING HANGED

Next morning, when we got up, the first thing I thought of was Owlyglass. "Will he get caught at last?" I said. "Maybe this time somebody will get the better of him, maybe have him put to death or something."

"No, no, no," said my brother. "Till always escapes, he's great."

"No, I'm not so sure," I said. "He got pretty close to it in that last place."

So by the time we were ready to go and see Horst, we were fairly bursting to find out what was going to happen.

We dashed into Horst's room, and there he was, sitting at the table as usual, one hand on the table, one hand on his knee.

I said, "Does he get caught today? Does he get caught?"

"Who?" said Horst.

"Till Owlyglass," I said.

"Never heard of him," said Horst.

"He has, hasn't he?" I said to my brother, but my brother was looking at something on the wall. Horst had hung our pictures there.

So my brother said to Horst, "Him on the wall."

"Oh yes, I remember," said Horst. "The king of Denmark."

"No, no, no," said my brother, "Till Owlyglass. You're only teasing us."

"All right, all right," said Horst. "I'll tell you what happened next."

* * *

The next place Till went to was a town called Lubeck, where he decided he'd have to be really careful and not get up to any of his usual tricks, because the people were very strict in Lubeck. And haven't I only just escaped being hanged in Luneburg? he thought to himself.

But we know Till, don't we? Even though he promised himself he wouldn't get up to any of his usual nonsense, in the end he couldn't stop himself. And this is what happened.

In Lubeck there was an innkeeper who was always boasting. He was a real show-off. He kept telling people that he was the wisest man in town, the man with the quickest brain. "I'm so quick," he said, "I'll never be caught out. No one will get the better of me."

When Till heard about this fellow, he thought he'd love to have a go at him. So he found two jugs, both exactly the same size, the same shape and the same colour. One of them he filled with water and the other he left empty. Then he hid the one full of water under his cloak and he took the empty jug into the inn and put it on the counter.

There he asked for a pint of wine, and the innkeeper filled Till's empty jug and put it on the counter.

Just then Till pretended he had tripped, and he deliberately knocked over a bottle that was standing on the counter. So of course the innkeeper bent down to pick up the pieces of the bottle. Now Till quickly swapped the jug full of wine with the jug full of water. So the jug full of wine was under his cloak and there was a jug full of water standing on the counter.

When the innkeeper had finished cleaning up the broken glass, Till asked, "How much is the wine?"

"Two shillings a pint and cheap at that, sir."

"You must be joking, mate," said Till. "Two shillings for this stuff!" And he took a sip of the water. "This is rubbish. I wouldn't give you more than one shilling for it. You might as well chuck it away, 'cos I'm not having it."

The innkeeper was really cross. "Look, my wine is high quality," he said. "If it's good enough for the Lord Mayor of this town, then it's good enough for you. And as for the price, it'd be cheap at three shillings, let alone two. I'm not going to let you have it for less, but if you can't pay up, then get out and I'll pour it back into my barrel."

But Till wouldn't go and he wouldn't pay, and this made the innkeeper even more angry. "Look, get out of here, you fool," he shouted. "You don't know what's good for you, idiot. Just get out of my shop, and don't hang about pestering honest, hard-working people."

In the end, Till shrugged his shoulders and left with the jug full of wine under his cloak. But just as he was going out of the door, he said, "I don't care if I am a fool. You ought to be more polite to people who come into your shop. And anyway, even the wisest men sometimes fall for tricks played by fools." Then he ran off down the street.

Of course the moment the innkeeper heard that, he guessed something was wrong, even if he didn't quite know what, so he shouted, "Stop thief! Stop thief!" and ran off up the road after Till.

Till ran as fast as he could, but a group of city constables heard the shouting and soon they were after him as well. It was one of them who caught him. They searched him and found the jug full of wine under his cloak.

The innkeeper was delighted. "Aha, you thought you could trick me, the sharpest fellow around," he crowed. "Nobody tricks me and gets away with it. You've had your little laugh, have you? You wait till I have you up before the judges.

They'll hang you for this, and I'll have the last laugh."

So Till was bound up and taken before the judges. Secretly, they were pleased the innkeeper had been tricked, but Till had broken the law and they were bound to pass sentence on him. "Till Owlyglass," the chief of the judges said, "you are guilty of stealing the innkeeper's wine. You are condemned to die." And Till was dragged off to prison, to await his execution.

* * *

Old Man Horst stopped there.

"You can't stop now," I said.

"No, that's all for today," said Horst.

"No, you can't leave it like that. We won't sleep, thinking about it."

"You really want to hear the awful truth, do you?"

"Yes, yes, yes," we said.

"All right," said Horst.

* * *

Poor Till sat in his little prison cell waiting for the hangman to take him to the gallows. But amazing though it may be, he didn't seem to mind. He sat there in the dark, as cheerful as ever, making fun of the guard.

"Hard luck, you're in prison," Till said to him.

"It's not me who's in prison," said the guard.

"Well," said Till, "I'll tell you something for nothing. You'll still be here after I've gone."

And of course he was right. The guard would still be there after Till was dead and gone.

On the last night before Till was due to die, the guard brought him his last meal. Till seemed to enjoy this meal more than usual.

"Hey, guard, what's the best meal in your life?" he asked.

"The next one," said the guard, thinking this would make Till unhappy.

"Oh, hard luck," said Till. "This is the best meal in my life, because I know I'll never have to eat such muck again."

The day of the execution was stormy and wet,

but in spite of this a huge crowd gathered to see Till die. Till was brought on a cart through the streets of Lubeck. Some people were sad, because they had laughed at his tricks, and they were pleased he had got the better of the innkeeper. But others were glad Till had been caught at last and this was his last day on earth.

Till passed the innkeeper and his friends, who shouted at him, "It just goes to show, no matter how clever you think you are, the law catches up with you in the end."

Till smiled and laughed, and someone called out, "What a shame it's a rainy day, Owlyglass."

"Don't worry about that," said Till. "I'm luckier than you, I won't get wet coming back in the rain."

At last the cart arrived at the special place where Till was to be hanged, and Till climbed up the ladder. The hangman put the rope round

Till's neck. Then Till turned to the crowd and said these words: "Lord Mayor, aldermen, merchants and townspeople of Lubeck. You have decided I must die, and so it must be. I don't ask you to pardon me. There's no point. I have always believed that we should all live short and happy lives, and that's what I've had, a short and happy life. But before I die I would like to ask for one last favour. I hope no one will deny me that."

The chief judge thought for a moment and then said, "Yes, it's true, it is an old custom to allow a sinner one last wish before he dies."

"But will my wish be granted?" said Till.

"I promise you that your wish will be granted," said the judge, "but only so long as you do not ask to live, you do not ask for anything that will make us late doing what we have to do to you, and so long as it doesn't cost us any money."

"You promise me on your honour, in front of

all these people of Lubeck, that you will carry out my wish?" said Till.

"We promise," said the judge. "What is your wish?"

"I would like every judge, the Lord Mayor and all his aldermen to come every morning for three days to where I am lying dead, and one by one I would like each of them to kiss my bum three times before breakfast."

When Till said this, there was uproar. People cheered and shouted and laughed. The judges and the Lord Mayor and the aldermen looked at one another. "Well, um, ah, that's not really fair, you know," they muttered.

"It doesn't matter if it's fair," said Till. "You promised."

And the crowd took up the cry. "You promised, you promised ..."

Of course, none of the judges or the aldermen

125

or the Lord Mayor wanted to kiss a dead man's bum three times before breakfast. And they knew that the people of Lubeck would make them keep their promise.

They quickly realised there was only one thing they could do. They would have to set Till free.

So, angrily and sadly, they had to take Till down from the scaffold and send him away, and off he went, grinning all over his face.

Even so, he made very sure never to show his grin in Lubeck, ever again.

* * *

"Phew," I said, "I don't believe it. He got away. I never thought he'd do it that time."

My brother was still laughing. "No one would kiss his bare bum."

"Now listen here," said Horst. "You keep that story to yourself. Don't go running around all over the place telling people about it. You'll get me into trouble for telling you rude stories."

"All right," said my brother, "we won't tell anyone."

But I knew that the moment we got back to England, my brother would tell all his friends that one.

"Now off you go," said Horst. And off we went.

THE NINTH DAY

WHEN WE HEAR HOW TILL OWLYGLASS
FILLED HIS POCKETS WITH MONEY,
MAKING BETS AT THE COURT OF
COUNT LIMBURG

Next day my brother said we had to play a trick on Horst because he hadn't given us our medicine yet.

"What kind of trick?" I said.

"Just you wait and see," said my brother.

Later on, as usual, we went down to see Horst. We went in and sat down and my brother said, "Look, Horst, I'm really sorry, but Mum and Dad said we can't come and see you any more. "

"Why's that?" said Horst.

"Well, I told them that story you told us yesterday about how Till escaped from being hanged, and my mum and dad were really cross about it."

Horst looked worried.

"They said we can't come and hear your stories any more."

Of course I knew my brother was making all this up, but Horst didn't and he looked really sad. I looked at my brother's face and I could see that the corners of his mouth were twitching a little, as if he was going to laugh any minute, so the corners of my mouth started twitching as well, and then I just burst out laughing. Well, when I started laughing, so did my brother.

So Horst said, "What's so funny?"

"I was only joking," said my brother. "I didn't really tell Mum and Dad and they didn't say we couldn't come any more."

"Oh good," said Horst, and I think he was really quite glad that it wasn't true. He had looked quite sad for a moment.

"Right," said Horst, rubbing his hands. "So I'll tell you some more."

* * *

Till was getting braver and braver. He thought now was the time to try out a few tricks on royal people, on kings, princes, counts and the like. So the next place he took himself to was Limburg, to see Count Limburg.

Everyone knew that Count Limburg was someone who liked to bet, and he always bet for money. "I bet you two hundred gold pieces that my horse is faster than yours," he'd say, or, "I bet you a hundred gold pieces I can eat more than you." Then he would have a horse race or an eating competition, and whoever won would win the money.

When Till heard about Count Limburg, he thought, I could do very well for myself up against this fellow. So he travelled to Limburg and presented himself at court.

The count had heard of Till and soon they were talking about Till's past adventures. Till told the count how he was baptised three times in one day and the count told Till how he was born in the middle of a thunderstorm.

"Of course," said Till, "that was how you got your birthmark."

"What birthmark?" said the count.

"The birthmark on your back," said Till.

"I haven't got a birthmark on my back," said the count.

"Yes, you have," said Till. "It's just underneath your shoulder blade. You just don't want to admit it, do you? I'll tell you what, I bet you ten pieces of silver you have a birthmark on your back just below your shoulder blade."

The count loved it. "Aha, just what I like," he

said. "A bet that I can't possibly lose. You've lost your money this time, Owlyglass. I'll prove to you straightaway you're wrong." At that, right in the middle of the court, the count took off his rich robes and showed Till his bare back. And he was right. There was no birthmark there at all.

"Well," said Till, "you're right and I'm wrong.

You've beaten me and here are your ten pieces of silver. But I'll tell you something, next time I see that servant of yours I'll be having a bit of a row with him."

"Why's that?" said the count.

"Because it was him who told me that you had that birthmark."

The count thought all this was really funny, and he stood there laughing at Till, the great trickster, getting it wrong.

"Never mind, Owlyglass," he said. "Don't look so sad about it. I enjoyed the bet." And he threw Till a purse of money.

In the evening, when it was time to go to bed, the count, as usual, ordered his servant to come and help him take off his robes. And he asked the servant, "Tell me, why in heaven's name did you tell poor Owlyglass that nonsense about me having a birthmark on my back? I've a good mind to give you the sack for making up such silly stories about me."

"I'm terribly sorry, sir, but you must be mistaken," the servant said. "I never said anything of the kind to Owlyglass. It's him who's lying."

"Then explain to me," said the count, "how come Owlyglass was so sure I had this birthmark? He even bet me ten pieces of silver that I had one. Of course I don't suppose he thought I'd take the bet. But I did, and I proved that he was wrong."

"Proved?" said the servant. "Proved? How do you mean, sir?"

"Oh, quite simple," said the count. "Right there and then, in the middle of the court, I took off my clothes and showed him."

"Oh no," moaned the servant. "You didn't, did you? Oh, the rogue, the cunning rascal!"

"What's the problem?" said the count.

"Only yesterday, your Owlyglass boasted to me that he could get you to take off your clothes in the middle of the court."

"So?" said the count. "There's nothing to get upset about."

"I said you'd never take your clothes off in court, so he bet me twenty pieces of silver that you would. I've lost my bet. He lost ten pieces of silver to you, but he's won twenty pieces off me. He's ten pieces of silver richer."

The count realised that Till had outwitted him. So the next day he went to Till and paid the servant's twenty pieces of silver.

"You've fooled me once, Owlyglass," he said, "but I'll beat you next time."

"All right," said Till, "let's try at once. I will make it easy for you. I will admit that I am the loser if you can repeat after me seven words without making a mistake."

"I'm not that stupid," said the count. "You think I can't say seven words after you? Look, I'll bet you fifty pieces of gold I can repeat any seven words you like."

"Right, " said Till, "we'll start right away. I give you..."

"I give you..." repeated the count.

"My best cloak," said Till.

"My best cloak," said the count.

"Wrong," said Till.

"Why?" said the count. "I said everything you said."

"Not every word," said Till. "Never mind, I'll give you another chance. I am ..."

"I am . . ." said the count.

"A great big fool," said Till.

"A great big fool," said the count.

"Wrong," said Till.

"No, I'm not wrong," said the count. "I've said

exactly what you said, even though you made me give away my best cloak and say I'm a fool. I said everything you said. You've lost the bet, not me."

"No, sir," said Till. "You lost. On both occasions you said six words after me, completely right, but my seventh word was 'wrong'. If you had said 'wrong', you'd have won."

The count didn't know whether to kick himself or kick Till, but either way he had to hand over the fifty pieces of gold.

The next day the count noticed that Till was looking a bit upset.

"What's the matter, Owlyglass?" he asked.

"Well, strange things are happening to me, sir," Till said.

"Like what?" said the count.

"Well," said Till, "I don't know what's wrong with me, but every time I go to the market there's a woman there who does something really strange. The moment she sees me she starts smashing up all the cups and bowls and plates that she's selling on her stall."

I don't believe this one, the count thought to himself. So he said, "But that's all the poor woman's got in the world, her cups and bowls and things. That's how she earns her money, selling them, so why would she smash them all up just because she sees you?"

"Exactly," said Till. "Why? That's what's worrying me."

There's a trick here, thought the count, but I can't figure out what. "I bet you ..." he said out loud to Till, "I bet you fifty pieces of gold that she doesn't smash up all her crockery the moment she sees you."

"Very well," said Till. "Let's go."

So the count and Till went off to the market.

When they got there, they saw the lady sitting in front of her bowls and plates and jugs and cups, looking very proud. She was doing very well, selling them to the people who had come into town. The count and Till moved a bit nearer. The lady caught sight of Till and immediately turned round, picked up a hammer and started attacking her pots. She went at it like mad,

banging and crashing with the hammer until every single piece of crockery on her stall was smashed into little bits.

Of course, the moment people started hearing the noise they came rushing up to see what was going on. Soon there was a huge crowd watching the woman.

The count couldn't believe his eyes. "Well, well, Owlyglass. You've won that bet as well, so here are your fifty pieces of gold. But I still don't understand why the woman does it. Is there something wrong with you, or what?"

"I can explain, sir. This morning, first thing, before you got up, I went to the market and said to the woman I'd give her enough money to pay for all her crockery, and ten pieces of gold on top of that, if she promised to do one thing for me."

"Oh yes," said the count, beginning to understand. "If she promised what?"

"The moment she saw me arrive at the market with you, sir, she should start smashing up her crockery."

"You've fooled me again, Owlyglass," said the count. "I've lost too much money betting with you."

"I don't think so," said Till.

"Well, I do," said the count, and he turned round and marched back to his court.

Till could see that the count was no longer amused. So as soon as he could, he slipped quietly away from Limburg, just in case things got a little too hot for him there.

* * *

"Where's he going to next?" I said.

"I think he's on his way to the famous city of Prague," said Horst.

"Who's he going to meet there?"

"Ah, this time he's going to meet the cleverest

people in the world. The great professors."

"He won't beat them," I said.

"He will," said my brother.

"Will he?" I said.

"Wait and see," said Horst.

"You always say that," I said.

"Don't be rude," said my brother, and off we went.

THE TENTH DAY

WHEN WE HEAR HOW TILL OWLYGLASS CAUSED AN INNKEEPER TO BE TERRIFIED BY A DEAD, FROZEN WOLF

Next day me and my brother started talking about Owlyglass as soon as we got up.

"He's on the way to Prague now," I said.

"He's not really going there now," said my brother. "Owlyglass lived hundreds of years ago."

"I know, I know, I know," I said.

"So he can't be going there now, can he?" my brother said.

"I know, I know, I know," I said. "But you know what I mean."

"Till isn't going anywhere," said my brother. "Horst is just telling us a story."

"Yes, but they're true stories," I said.

"No, they're not," said my brother. "He's just making them up."

"No, he isn't," I said. "They're stories about someone who really lived."

"Rubbish," said my brother.

"All right, we'll ask Horst. He'll tell us," I said.

And that's what we did.

"Are the Owlyglass stories true?" I said to Horst.

"It all depends what you mean by true," said Horst.

"Did they really happen?" I said.

"Listen," said Horst. "I believe they happened and the man who told me the stories believed they happened. Does that make them true?"

"Yes," I said.

"No, it doesn't," said my brother. "Because the man who told the man who told could have been lying."

"But he wasn't lying, was he?" I said.

"He might have been," said Horst, "and then again, he might not have been."

"I can't stand this," I said. "Just tell us another story, please, Horst. What happens next?"

* * *

Till was on his way to Prague and it was winter. There was no time Till hated more than cold winter nights. In the summer he could sleep out in the open, or find a barn and sleep in the hay. But in winter he had to tramp along the road all day, his feet getting frozen, hoping to find an inn where he could sit and warm himself by a big roaring fire. Of course, if he did find an inn, he could sit there and tell people all the funny things that had happened to him. And perhaps he could try out a trick or two on them.

One evening, after a long cold walk through the snow and wind, he came to an inn in the town of Eisleben. The innkeeper was another boastful man, who kept saying how brave he was. Till went in and sat down by the fire.

Not long after, three more travellers came in out of the dark cold night.

"What time do you call this?" the innkeeper said. "Where have you lot been that keeps you out so late? Or have you been hanging about on the road or something?"

The travellers said, "Keep your temper, innkeeper. A wolf was lying in wait for us by the side of the road through the forest and we had to deal with him. In the end we were able to fight him off, but that's why we're a bit late."

When the innkeeper heard this, he burst out laughing. "You were held up by one single little wolf? I tell you, if I met *two* wolves while I was out I would deal with them single-handed and finish them off. And there wouldn't be much

left of them, I can tell you. And there you were, three of you, and you were scared of one single silly little wolf." The innkeeper went on and on laughing at the three travellers.

All the time Till sat by the fire listening. In the end it was time for bed, and Till slipped into the room where the three of them were sitting talking.

"We'll have to think of some way of dealing with this awful man," one of them was saying, "so that he doesn't bother us any more."

So Till said, "Look, friends, I think our inn keeper is all talk. Listen to me and I don't think he'll ever boast about wolves again."

Of course the travellers were really pleased to listen. They promised they'd give Till some money if he could do what he said, and more than that, they'd pay his bill.

"This is what you've got to do," said Till. "Tomorrow you must leave the inn, go about your business and then when you've finished, just come back again, as normal. I'll be here as well and you'll see, I'll make him shut his mouth about this wolf affair."

The travellers agreed, and the next day, off

they went, paying their bill and Till's as well.

As they went, the innkeeper called after them, "Mind how you go, chaps. Make sure no big beastly wolf scares you on your way," and he fell about laughing.

And the travellers said, "Thanks very much, innkeeper. Mind you, if the wolves eat us then we won't be coming here again, will we?"

Till left the same day. He hunted down a wolf, killed it and covered it with snow and ice until it was frozen hard. Then he made his way back to the inn, hiding the dead wolf in a big sack. The travellers were already back at the inn, and the innkeeper was still going on about the wolf. "Three men and one wolf, what brave chaps you are. I tell you, if I met two wolves, I would grab one by the throat till it died and at the same time cut the other one to pieces." And so he went on until bedtime.

Till kept quiet all the while. Then, just as before, he crept up to the travellers' room and said, "Gentlemen, don't put your light out yet, all right?"

When the innkeeper was safely in bed and the whole inn was quiet, Till crept out of his own room. He took the dead, frozen wolf out of the sack and carried it into the kitchen. He propped it upright, stuck two children's shoes into its mouth then nipped back into the travellers' room.

A few minutes later Till called out loudly for the innkeeper, "Innkeeper! Innkeeper! Hey, innkeeper!"

The innkeeper, half-asleep, called out, "What do you want?"

"Send the maid to fetch us a drink or we'll die of thirst," Till shouted.

The innkeeper wasn't happy about it. "For

goodness' sake, you lot, drinking day and night, you'll drive me mad!" But he sent for the maid all the same, to fetch them a drink.

The maid got up, went down to the kitchen, and there was the wolf! Terrified, she saw the shoes in its mouth and thought it had eaten the children, and now it would eat her. She rushed out of the inn, and hid behind a barrel in the yard.

A few minutes later Till called out again, "Innkeeper! Innkeeper! Where's our drink? What's keeping you?"

Now the innkeeper called the man-servant, not knowing what had happened to the maid. And when the servant went downstairs to the kitchen he saw the wolf and thought it had eaten the maid and the children, so he dashed off in a panic and hid in the cellar.

Now Till turned to the travellers and said,

"Hang on, lads, it's the innkeeper's turn next and we're in for a really good laugh." Then he called out, "Innkeeper! Innkeeper! Where's that drink, in heaven's name? We're dying of thirst here. If the maid and the man-servant can't fetch it, fetch it yourself, will you?"

The innkeeper was furious. "You people make me sick with your constant drinking. Drink, drink, drink – it's all work for me, you know!"

But even so, up he got and went downstairs. And there was the wolf with the children's shoes in its jaw. He rushed upstairs straight into the travellers' room.

"Come quick! Quick!" he cried. "Help me, help! Downstairs in the kitchen there's a terrible beast! It's eaten the children, the maid and the man-servant! What am I going to do?"

So Till and the travellers crept downstairs with the innkeeper. When they went into the kitchen,

Till walked over to the wolf and gave it a kick, so that it fell over with a bang. Then he called the maid from the yard and the man-servant from the cellar, and he turned to the innkeeper and said, "Look at it! The wolf is dead. And there's you, screaming your head off. What a scared

little fellow you are. Do you think a dead wolf's going to bite you? But hang on – wasn't it you last night who was so brave that one wolf wouldn't be enough for you to have a fight with? Weren't you the man who said you needed two wolves to prove yourself?"

When the innkeeper heard this from Till, he crept back to his room. He felt so ashamed that he had been scared of a dead, frozen wolf.

But the travellers loved it. They laughed and they laughed and gave Till a purse full of money and took him with them on the way to Prague.

* * *

"Is that all?" I said.

"Yes," said Horst.

"But Till hasn't got to Prague yet. You said we'd hear about Prague."

"But he's got to get there first," said Horst.

"Can we hear about it now?" I said.

"Oh no, the Prague story will take much too long," said Horst. "No more stories today. Off you go and mind the snake on the stairs."

"What snake?" I said.

"He's only joking," my brother said, and off we went.

THE ELEVENTH DAY

WHEN WE HEAR HOW TILL OWLYGLASS
PROVED HIMSELF WISER THAN
THE WISEST PROFESSORS OF PRAGUE,
AND HOW HE TAUGHT A DONKEY
TO READ

The next day we knew that Till was going to get to Prague to see those clever people.

"That man with the wine caught Till out, so I suppose all those professors will," said my brother.

"Till will think of some way to trick them," I said. "Maybe he'll invent some machine."

When it was time to see Horst, we went straight in and said, "Prague."

Horst looked up. "Prague? What's Prague? Is this a new way to say hello? Prague!"

"No, no, no," said my brother. "It's where Till's going next, isn't it?"

"You're right," said Horst. "He went to Prague, to see the professors."

* * *

At long last, after many days' travel, Till arrived in the famous city of Prague. In those days all of Europe knew about Prague, because it was packed full of the world's cleverest professors, scholars and students.

Till stood in a doorway and watched the clever people walking down the narrow streets in their long gowns saying all sorts of clever things to one another, using long words like hypothesis and Aristotle. And of course Till had a thought, an Owlyglass thought. And you know and I know what that means – trouble!

That night Till went round every church door sticking up posters. On the posters he had written, "Till Owlyglass is the wisest man in the world. Till Owlyglass will answer any questions the wisest men of Prague want to ask him."

In the morning the great masters who worked at Prague University saw Till's posters. They were furious.

"What a cheek!" they said.

"How dare he?" they asked.

So they all met together in one of the great halls.

"Gentlemen," said one, "the answer to this problem is simple. We invite this fool Owlyglass to come to our university. Because he is so afraid of our great minds, he will be afraid to come. Then everyone will know that he is an idiot."

"But what if he does come?" asked another.

"Then we will ask him such clever questions that he can't possibly answer them," said a third.

The professors were sure they could make

a fool of Till. So a great hall was prepared, hundreds of people came, a messenger was sent to ask Till to come ... and Till came.

He walked into the hall with that grin on his face.

"Afternoon, professors," said Till. "Let's have you, then! First question! What is it?"

The professors were amazed that Till had come. But once they had calmed down, the head of the university, the chancellor, began. "Our first question is, how many gallons of water are there in all of the seven seas?"

The crowd gasped, but Till answered at once. "Eight hundred thousand billion, two hundred and twenty-six million, four hundred and eighty-nine thousand, six hundred and twenty-eight gallons!"

"Are there?" said the chancellor.

"Yes," said Till, "and if you don't believe me,

stop the rivers running into your seven seas and measure it yourself."

"Well," said the chancellor, "I ... er ... can't do ...er ... at this moment ... er . . .I ... er ..."

"Right," said Till, over the applause of the

crowd, "next question, then."

The professor of history stood up and asked, "Tell me, how many days have there been since the world began?"

"Seven," said Till. "Monday, Tuesday, Wednesday, Thursday, Friday, Saturday and Sunday. I haven't missed out any, have I?"

"No," said the professor, "but ..."

"So I'm right, aren't I?" said Till. "Next question."

The crowd clapped wildly, until the professor of geography asked, "Where is the centre of the world?"

"Here," said Till, "here, where I'm standing."

"How do you know?" said the professor.

"Get a bit of string," said Till, "and measure round the world. You'll soon see."

"Well," said the professor, "I ... er ... can't, I'm not ... um ..."

"Next question," said Till, and the crowd rose, cheering, to their feet.

The same professor now asked, "How far is the earth from heaven?"

"Not far," said Till.

"What do you mean, not far?" said the professor.

"Look, you go to heaven," said Till. "I will call up to you from down here. If you can hear me, it's not far. If you can't hear me, it's far and I'm wrong."

"This is preposterous," said the professor, but the crowd were all on Till's side.

"Any more questions?" said Till.

What could the professors say? Not one of them could think of another question to ask.

So off went Till, grinning all over his face, leaving the professors speechless and the crowd cheering him all the way.

The professors were furious and sat about shouting at one another for days. They knew that Till had made them look like fools. Then one wily old professor came up with a plan.

"Gentlemen," he said, "I think we should send Till a letter like this. 'Great Master Till Owlyglass, you have shown us that you are a very clever man, in fact so clever we think you could teach anyone. Let us find a pupil and all you have to do to prove yourself is to teach this pupil how to read.'"

And that was the letter Till received.

"Yes," said Till. "Bring me who you like, I will teach them to read."

The next day the pupil arrived. The professors sent Till a little grey donkey.

"Here you are, Great Master Owlyglass," they said. "Here is your pupil." And they stood about giggling.

"Thank you, friends," said Till. "Can you give me a little time to do the job?"

"Of course," said the professors.

So Till took the little donkey to the stable of the inn where he was staying and off went the

professors, still giggling. They were sure they had fooled Till this time.

Now Till went to the bookbinders and bought a book with no words in it. And afterwards he went back to the inn and on each page of the book he painted some letters. And he sent for the professors again, and back they came.

"He can't have done it," said one.

"No one can teach a donkey to read," said another.

"The man's an idiot," said a third.

"Gentlemen," said Till, leading the professors into the stable. "My pupil can't read many words yet, but he's made a start. Let me show you."

Till led the donkey up to the book and slipped a few oats between the pages.

The donkey got excited and began to look for the oats, turning the pages of the book. As he turned them, he brayed, "Eee-arr, eee-arr, eee-arr."

And what Till had painted on the pages of the book were the letters E and R.

"Eee-arr, eee-arr, eee-arr!" the donkey went on.

"There," said Till. "He's a bit slow, but he's

coming on, the clever little fellow, don't you think? Give me a bit more time and I'll soon have him reading fluently."

The professors did not know where to look, or what to say. So they wrapped their long gowns around themselves and hurried out of the stable. Till had certainly taught them a lesson.

* * *

"That's brilliant," said my brother, and he sat there thinking. Then he took out a piece of paper and wrote something on it. He held it up for Horst to look at.

"What does this say, Horst?" my brother asked.

Horst read it out loud. "It says, 'Do not read this. If you do, you are crazy.'"

"You read it, you read it." said my brother. "You're crazy."

"But I didn't read out that it said *I'm* crazy," Horst answered. "It said *you're* crazy."

I burst out laughing, "He's right, you know, he's right, you know."

Then my brother got all ratty and said it was time to go and Horst winked at me as we went out.

THE TWELFTH DAY

WHEN WE HEAR HOW TILL OWLYGLASS
CURED A SMALL BOY'S CONSTIPATION,
AND HOW HE TAUGHT A MERCHANT
TO PACK EGGS TIGHTLY

The next day my brother said it was nearly the end of the holiday and maybe Horst wouldn't have time to tell us all the Owlyglass stories.

So when we went to see Horst, the first thing we asked him was if he'd have time to tell us all the stories.

"I can only tell you the stories I know," said Horst. "But maybe there are some people who know hundreds of other stories about Owlyglass."

"But will you have time to tell us all the stories *you* know?" I said.

"I think so," said Horst, "but we'll have to hurry up."

"Good," said my brother. "Where's Till going now?"

"He's off to Hessen to see a kind of prince called a landgrave. Can you say that?"

"A landgrave," I said.

"Good," said Horst. "But before he gets there he gets up to one or two tricks on the way."

* * *

In one of the inns where he stayed on the way to Hessen, Till saw a little boy who was ill in bed. He was the landlady's little boy. He was only three. So Till asked the landlady what was the matter with him.

"Oh dear," said the landlady, "he's constipated. He won't sit on the potty and do his business. He hasn't done one for a whole week! If only we could make him go, I think he'd get better."

"I know just the thing for him," said Till.

"Do you?" said the landlady. "Oh, if you can help my poor little boy, you can have whatever you want."

"Just leave it to me, landlady," said Till. "I'll make him better."

So the landlady went out into the garden to cut a cabbage, and while she was out, Till sat on the little boy's potty and did a big one. Then he pulled up his trousers, sat the little boy on the potty and called for the landlady.

"Landlady, we're ready," he said.

The landlady came in, saw her little boy sitting on the potty and took a quick look to see if he had done anything.

"Oh, he has," she said. "But, oh dear, no wonder he couldn't go, poor little fellow. But you've made him better, bless you, Mr Owlyglass. What a clever man you are!"

"Not really," said Till, pretending to be shy.

"But how did you do it?" said the landlady. "How did you make him better?"

"Aha," said Till, tapping the side of his nose. "That's a secret, ma'am, but next time I come this way, perhaps I'll tell you."

"What can I give you in return, then?" she asked. That day Till had money in his pocket and he was happy enough just to enjoy the joke without taking anything from the landlady. And, as it happened, the little boy soon got better, so the landlady never knew she had been tricked. She always thought that it was Till who had cured him. And who knows, perhaps it was.

In this same inn Till met a merchant who bought butter, cream and milk from farmers, and took it to market to sell. He sold it for more than he paid for it, and that's how he made his living. He was a very greedy and stupid man, and Till got interested in him, and told him he would like to help.

"Why? What can you do for me?" the merchant asked.

"I have a few ideas about how you could

make more money," said Till.

"Oh really," said the merchant. "How?"

"To start with," said Till, "you could buy and sell eggs as well."

"Maybe this fellow does know a thing or two," thought the merchant, so he took Till on.

The next day they went round the farms buying milk and cream and butter. Till watched the merchant beating the farmers down.

"I'll give you five shillings for it," the merchant said.

"But if that's all you give me," said the farmer, "I won't have enough to feed my children."

"Five, and no more," the merchant insisted, and so the deal was done.

Now Till told the merchant, "Ask to buy some of his eggs!" And so the cart was soon piled high with baskets of butter, churns of milk, cans of cream and for the first time, nearly a hundred eggs.

As Till and the merchant were going down the road, Till said, "Look, master. Between each egg there's a gap, a space. Do you see what I mean?"

The merchant looked at the eggs in the basket and he saw what Till meant. Each egg was resting on another, but of course they didn't fit close together like bricks, because they were oval-shaped.

The merchant said, "You're right, son, you're right. There are spaces. Quite big spaces."

"You know what that means, don't you?" said Till.

"What?" the merchant asked.

"If we could squeeze the eggs together," Till said, "we'd get more in. Then you could sell more and you'd make more money."

The merchant's eyes lit up. "But how could I squeeze them together?" he asked.

"Just the same as you do with cabbages," said Till.

"How's that then?" said the merchant. He was beginning to think how lucky he was, employing a man like Till, who knew so much.

"What you do with cabbages," said Till, "is tread on them to squeeze them up closer and that way you get more in the basket."

"Oh, fine," said the merchant.

At the next village the merchant bought some more eggs from the farmers. Then he stood on top of the baskets and started treading on the eggs. Stamp, stamp, stamp he went, all over them. And of course the eggs broke, there were whites and yolks and shells all over the place, and still he went on stamping.

All the people of the village were standing round laughing at the merchant.

"What are you doing?" they asked. "Why

are you stamping on the eggs?"

"I'm just squeezing them together so that I can get more in the basket," he answered, which just made them laugh all the more.

Bit by bit it dawned on the merchant that he was doing the wrong thing. He stopped what he was doing and looked at his legs all covered in egg, yellow up to the knees. Someone's made a fool of me, he thought.

The merchant looked for Till, but he was nowhere to be seen.

Then one of the people standing there, laughing, said, "Hey, you know who that fellow was, who was helping you pack more eggs in your basket?"

"No," said the merchant.

"Till Owlyglass," said the man.

"Oh no," said the merchant. "Oh no. If I lay my hands on him I'll ..."

But it was no good. Till was away down the road heading for Hessen and the landgrave of Hessen, the man who wanted everyone to think that he was a prince.

* * *

"Can you tell us that one now?" I asked.

"No, I'll tell you tomorrow," said Horst. "I've got things to do."

"What are you having for lunch today, Horst?" my brother asked.

"Oh pork and potatoes, I think," Horst said.

"Why don't you have scrambled eggs?" my brother said.

"Get along with you now, you two," said Horst, and off we went.

THE THIRTEENTH DAY

WHEN WE HEAR HOW TILL OWLYGLASS
PAINTED THE ANCESTORS OF THE
LANDGRAVE OF HESSEN, AND HOW LIARS
COULD NOT SEE WHAT HE PAINTED

The next day, we knew we were going to get the story about this man called the landgrave.

"Was he a prince, did Horst say?" asked my brother.

"I think he said he wanted everyone to think he was a prince," I said.

"I wonder what Till's going to do with him. Maybe he's going to dress up as a princess," said my brother.

By the time we got to see Horst, we had convinced ourselves that Till was going to dress up as a princess and ask to marry the landgrave.

So I said to Horst, "Does Till become a princess today?"

Horst looked at me as if I was mad. "No," he said, "he's going to see the landgrave of Hessen. That's what today's story is about."

* * *

Till had heard that the landgrave of Hessen was forever boasting about his royal blood. He said his father had been a prince, and so was he – in fact his entire family was royal. But Till knew that the landgrave was a liar, and a very rich and very stupid one at that.

Till arrived at the landgrave's castle in the town of Marburg.

"Lord," said Till, "I am an artist."

"Oh, that's wonderful," said the landgrave. "We love artists here. What sort of work do you do?"

"Sir," said Till, "I am a painter. I am the world's

greatest painter, my paintings are better than anyone else's."

"Oh, that's wonderful," said the landgrave again. "Can I see some of your work?"

"Of course," said Till, and he opened up his bag and took out some paintings he had bought in Flanders.

"Oh, that's wonderful," said the landgrave. "Look, er, painter, sir, how much would you charge to paint on the wall of our castle hall the story of the landgraves of Hessen? How I made friends with the King of Hungary, Prince Whatshisname, Lord Thingummy and the Duke of er ... um ..."

"Well, gracious Prince," Till replied, "if you want a really excellent job done, it'll cost you four hundred gold pieces."

"Oh, that's wonderful," said the landgrave.

Till said he needed one hundred gold pieces

right away to buy paints and the landgrave agreed. Then Till said he needed something else.

"What I need," he said, "is complete peace and quiet while I am working. I don't want anyone to come in where I am working or even ask if they can come in."

"Oh, yes," said the landgrave, "that's fine, that's wonderful."

So Till took over the castle hall, and no one ever disturbed him or came in to look, and he worked for one, two, three, four weeks.

By now the landgrave was dying to see how his painting was getting on. He kept wondering, would it really be as good as the paintings Till had shown him when he first came to the castle?

At last the landgrave shouted through the door, "Oh, master painter, sir, I really would like to come in and see how my painting is coming on." And Till came out to see him.

"Landgrave, sir," Till said, "you can come and look now. But first, I must tell you a secret about the painting. Some people will not be able to see it. They'll look at it but they'll see nothing."

"What kind of people?" asked the landgrave.

"Liars," said Till. "Liars won't be able to see my painting at all."

"Oh, that's wonderful," said the landgrave, though he did wonder, just a little, if his lies about his royal family would mean he wouldn't be able to see the painting.

Till took the landgrave into the hall. A pair of curtains covered the painting. Now, with the landgrave, Till drew the curtains aside. The wall was completely bare.

"Most noble landgrave," said Till, "look at this marvellous painting, with its wealth of detail and beautiful colours. See here, in this corner, I have painted the very first Prince of Hessen. See here,

how one of your forefathers met the Pope. And here's the Princess of Bavaria, who married the Emperor Adolphus, and his son Prince William, and all the princes all the way down to your good self, sir. Here, sir, in this one painting, the whole story of the Hessens is told. Who could do anything but admire it?"

The landgrave looked and looked but he couldn't see a thing. He thought to himself, All I can see is the wall but I had better not say anything to this painter fellow or he'll know that I've lied about my family.

So instead the landgrave said, "Oh, that's wonderful. Clever, clever, master painter, you've done a wonderful painting, though I have to say I am not an ... er ... um ... expert. But now I must go..."

That same day the landgrave's wife asked him, "How's the painting? Have you seen what he's done? Are you pleased? To be honest I'm not sure he's going to do much. I have a funny feeling he isn't quite who he says he is."

But the landgrave replied, "Oh no, I trust him and he's shown himself to be very skilful. He's a great master of the brush, dear. Would you like to take a look?"

"Yes, indeed," said the landgrave's wife.

So Till was sent for and he agreed to let her look at the painting. He told her, as he had told the landgrave, what kind of people would not be able to see it. In she went and with her went eight servants and her woman-jester. Once again Till drew the curtains and started describing all the forefathers and princes and royal families. Of course nobody could see anything. But did they speak up? Did they say they couldn't see the painting? No, not one of them.

Then suddenly the woman-jester said, "Oh well, I suppose I'm one of your liars, I can't see a thing."

Oh dear, thought Till, Trouble here. The fool is speaking the truth. I'd better get out, and quickly!

When the landgrave next saw his wife, he asked her, "Did you like the painting? What did you think of it?"

"My Gracious Lord," she said, "I thought it was marvellous. Though I have to say my woman-jester didn't like it. She said she couldn't see a thing. Actually, my servants and my jester all think there's something funny going on."

The landgrave sent a message to Till, telling him to finish off the painting as soon as possible.

The moment Till got the message, he went to see the landgrave's treasurer. He took his three hundred gold pieces and left.

The next day the landgrave called for Till, and then he heard that Till had gone. So he went with all his lords to look at the painting. They looked and they looked, but of course they didn't see a thing. But again, did anybody say anything? Did anyone say they couldn't see it? No.

Then somebody noticed something in the corner.

"What's that?" said one of the lords.

They drew closer and saw that it was a little drawing of an owl and a looking glass. An owl and a glass. Owlyglass.

The landgrave lifted his hands in the air. "Oh no, this is the work of Till Owlyglass," he said. "We've been tricked. There is no painting here."

Everyone in the hall looked at one another. "Of course, quite right, there isn't a painting there," they muttered.

Then the landgrave spoke up. "For one moment, I thought I couldn't see the painting because I'm a ... well, never mind what I thought I was. Now we all know why we can't see a painting here, don't we?"

"Yes, of course we do," said everyone and they felt much better now they knew they weren't liars. There were some people, though, who remembered that they and the landgrave had pretended they could see Till's wonderful picture. It was then that they realised Till was right: people who lie couldn't see his painting. You see, Till showed more of the landgrave and his court on that bare wall than any real picture could have done.

* * *

Horst stopped.

"And, and, and," said my brother.

"And what?" said Horst.

"And meanwhile Till was running down the road with three hundred gold pieces in his pocket, and, and, and ..." said my brother.

"I know what," I said, "and grinning all over his face."

"You're going home tomorrow, aren't you?" said Horst.

"Oh yes," I said. "Have you got more stories to tell us?"

"I might have," said Horst.

"Oh no," said my brother. "We won't have enough time."

"Come and say goodbye, all the same," said Horst.

"And we'll get our medicine then, won't we?" I said.

"Maybe," said Horst, smiling, and off we went.

THE FOURTEENTH DAY

WHEN WE HEAR HOW TILL OWLYGLASS
KEPT UP HIS TRICKS EVEN ON
HIS DEATHBED, AND WHAT A
CURIOUS EVENT TOOK PLACE
AT HIS FUNERAL

The next day was the last day of the holiday. Instead of rushing down to see Horst as soon as we could, we had to start packing. Then there was dinner and we knew that not long after that, we'd have to catch the train home.

Finally, when we had done everything we had to do, we went down to see Horst.

We went into that little room. I was a bit sad. I thought maybe this was going to be the last time we'd ever see Horst.

So I went up to him and said, "Thanks for the

stories, Horst," and I gave him a little kiss on the side of his face.

My brother said, "I don't think you've got time to tell us any more. We're going now."

"Oh well," Horst kept saying.

Then my brother said, "The medicine. Have you got the medicine?"

"The medicine?" said Horst. "I've already given it to you."

"No, you haven't," said my brother. "You know, the medicine to stop us being bad."

"Well," said Horst, "have you been bad for the last, let me see, fourteen days?"

"No," said my brother. "We've been coming to see you."

"There you are, then," said Horst. "You've had the medicine."

"No, come on, Horst," said my brother.

"Look here," said Horst. "Whatever it is I've

given you over these last fourteen days has stopped you being bad, hasn't it?"

"And being bored," I said.

"Oh, I see," said my brother. "I see."

"Good," said Horst.

"I don't," I said.

Then we said goodbye and shook hands and off we went on the long journey back to England. On the way back we stayed at a friend's house in Holland, so it was about a week before we got home. When we got there, a letter was waiting for us. It was from Horst. It went like this:

Dear Boys,

I told you many adventures about our friend Till Owlyglass and there are hundreds I don't know; but there is one more I had to tell you, so I've written it down.

For many, many years Till wandered all over

Germany and the countries around it, until he was very old; and then one day he fell seriously ill. He was in the town of Mollen at the time. In those days anyone who was dying used to talk to a priest. They told the priest about anything wrong they had ever done, so that the priest could pardon them. And that would give them the chance of going to heaven when they died.

So a priest came to see Till.

But this priest was very greedy. He loved money and he loved food and drink. When he saw that Till was a man of the world, a man who had travelled and seen many places, he guessed that here was a chance to make a bit of money.

"My son," the priest said to Till, "think of the peace of your soul after you die, think of the money you could give to the church for a mass to be sung for you after you die."

Till said, "Many thanks, Father, you've spoken

very wisely to me. Come back this afternoon and I'll have something for you."

So the priest went away, and Till fetched a jug and filled it with muck out of the gutter. On the top he put a few layers of gold pieces, so that you couldn't see the muck.

In the evening the priest came back. He listened to Till's confession, pardoned him and then said, "Do you have any thing to give the church, my son?"

So Till said, "Yes, Father. In that jug over there is some treasure. Put your hand in and take a coin or two. But don't dip your hand in too deep, will you, Father?"

"Thank you, my son," said the priest and he went over to the jug. Greedy as ever, he stuck his hand deep into the jug, and when he pulled it out again, it was covered with filth and muck.

Till sat up in his bed, laughing his head off;

and then he said, "I warned you not to dip too deep, you old greedy guts, but you couldn't stop yourself, could you?" And the priest rushed off, furious that he had been caught out.

Though Till was growing more sick and feeble by the hour, even this was not his last trick. In the final moments of his life, he called to his bedside some of his friends, the Lord Mayor of Mollen and the proper priest of Mollen.

"Gentlemen," he said, "I am dividing my treasure between you. Friends, you shall have one third. Lord Mayor, you shall have one third, to pay off the bills in Mollen. Father, you shall have one third for the church. You can have this money if you promise one thing – you will bury me in a proper churchyard, and you will sing and say a mass so that my soul may be saved."

"Yes," they all agreed, "we promise."

"Four weeks after I am gone," Till said with his final breath, "you can open my trunk. It's locked with three keys. Friends, here is one of them. Lord Mayor, here is another. And, Father, here is the third."

And then, at last, Till died.

Four weeks later Till's friends, the Lord Mayor and the priest all came together to open the trunk. The trunk was huge and weighed so much that it took several men to lift it. It seemed like it was full to the top with treasure. Everyone started getting excited, thinking how rich they were soon going to be. They used the three keys to unlock the trunk; they lifted the huge lid; they looked inside; and they found ... stones. Nothing but stones.

Within minutes they were shouting at one another.

"It was you! You've been here before and taken it!"

"It wasn't me, it was you! You did what you're saying I did!"

And they argued and fought until in the end one of them said, "Hang on, perhaps Till was telling us something. After all, what are jewels, if not stones? The best things in life are good health and happiness, aren't they? Not money. Not treasure."

But even this wasn't quite the last of Till's tricks. On the day of Till's funeral, when his coffin was being lowered into the grave, one of the ropes broke. Down dropped one end of the coffin and up came the other end, so that the coffin stood upright in the grave.

All the people standing there were amazed and

they called out, "Leave him like that, if he wants it that way. All his life he did strange things; so he can be strange even now, when he's dead."

Then they filled in the grave, and on Till's headstone they carved an owl holding a looking glass in its claws. And on the stone they wrote these words:

Till Owlyglass stands beneath this stone
With a grin on his face and all alone.

And that was the end of Till. And in another way it was the beginning, because since then people have never stopped telling stories about him.

Till Owlyglass, Till Eulenspiegel, the owl with the mirror in his hand. I often wonder what that means. Maybe Till was a kind of wise owl, who held up a mirror to everybody. Whoever looked in the mirror could see all the foolish things they did.

All the best, boys. Hope you liked the medicine. Hope to see you again one day. Love, Horst.

* * *

I never did see Horst again, but I've always remembered his stories. So I thought what I'd do is write them all down for you. I hope you liked them as much as I did.

ABOUT THE AUTHOR

Michael Rosen has written many
popular stories and poems for children,
including *We're Going on a Bear Hunt*.
He received the Eleanor Farjeon Award for
distinguished services to children's literature
in 1997, and was the Children's Laureate
from 2007 to 2009. A distinguished critic
and academic, he is a professor in the
Department of Education Studies at
Goldsmith's, University of London.
He is often called upon to talk about
children's literature and his poetry readings
are adored by children and adults. He also
presents radio programmes for the BBC.
Michael lives in London with his family.

ABOUT THE ILLUSTRATOR

Fritz Wegner studied at St Martin's
School of Art and began working as a
freelance illustrator after the war.
He illustrated his first book in 1950.
An extraordinarily talented artist, he has
worked with many celebrated authors,
including Allan Ahlberg, Leon Garfield,
Dorothy Sayers and Andre Maurois.
He lives in Highgate, North London.

First published 1990
by Walker Books Ltd
87 Vauxhall Walk,
London SE11 5HJ

This edition published 2014

2 4 6 8 10 9 7 5 3 1

Text © 1990 Michael Rosen
Illustrations © 1990 Fritz Wegner

The right of Michael Rosen and Fritz Wegner to be
identified as author and illustrator respectively of this work
has been asserted by them in accordance with the
Copyright, Designs and Patents Act 1988

This book has been typeset in Stemple Sneidler

Printed and bound in Great Britain by Clays Ltd, St Ives plc

British Library Cataloguing in Publication Data:
a catalogue record for this book is available from the British Library

ISBN 978-1-4063-4917-7

www.walker.co.uk